PRAISE FOR

"Funny, sexy, perfection. *Beautiful Bastard*."

—*Adriane Leigh, USA Today Bestselling Author*

"Not only is Blakemeister back, but he's on fire!! . . . I cannot believe how even more beyond uniquely quirky, smooth, and honestly in a class of its own L'Amour's writing style is."

—*A is For Alpha, B is for Books Blog*

"The *THAT MAN* series keeps getting better and better, funnier and sexier. Bravo, Nelle! No wonder this series is a runaway success!"

—*Arianne Richmonde, USA Today Bestselling Author*

"Blake Burns . . . the most funny and charming boyfriend next to Andrew Parrish and Drew Evans"

—*Bedtime Reads*

"Mr. Burns is the epitome of sex on a stick. Irresistible and naughty. Perfection! And get ready to die of laughter too."

—*G The Book Diva Blog*

"*THAT MAN* has everything readers could want. A funny and sexy read. Phenomenal!"

—*The Fairest of All Book Reviews*

"This is a 5-star book in a 5-star series and is sure to make you melt. Blake Burns lights up the pages with his Alpha attitude. He'll leave you screaming, 'MORE!'"

—*Random Musesomy*

Be prepared for another hot, sexy, and humorous read."
—*Love Between the Sheets Book Blog*

"The chemistry between Blake and Jennifer is so hot your Kindle will melt."

—*SubClub Books*

"Is it possible to love Blake even more than I did? A resounding YES!"

—*Goodreads Reviewer*

"Nelle L'Amour's writing is the perfect mixture of sexy dialogue, relatable characters, and laugh out-loud moments. Get ready to fall in love with *THAT MAN* all over again."

—*Vanessa Booke, USA Today Bestselling Author*

BOOKS BY NELLE L'AMOUR

Secrets and Lies
Sex, Lies & Lingerie
Sex, Lust & Lingerie
Sex, Love & Lingerie

Unforgettable
Unforgettable Book 1
Unforgettable Book 2
Unforgettable Book 3

THAT MAN Series
THAT MAN 1
THAT MAN 2
THAT MAN 3
THAT MAN 4
THAT MAN 5
THAT MAN 6
THAT MAN 7
THAT MAN 8

Alpha Billionaire Duet
TRAINWRECK 1
TRAINWRECK 2

Love Duet
Undying Love
Endless Love

A Standalone Romantic Comedy
Baby Daddy

A Second Chance Romantic Suspense Standalone
Remember Me

An OTT Insta-love Standalone
The Big O

A Romance Compilation
Naughty Nelle

THAT MAN 8

THAT MAN 8

NEW YORK TIMES BESTSELLING AUTHOR
NELLE L'AMOUR

Copyright © 2020 by Nelle L'Amour
Print Edition
All rights reserved worldwide

This is a work of fiction. Names, characters, places, and incidents are either the product of the author's imagination or used fictitiously. Any resemblance to events, locales, business establishments, or actual persons—living or dead—is purely coincidental.

No part of this book may be reproduced, uploaded to the Internet, or copied without permission from the author. The author respectfully asks that you please support artistic expression and help promote anti-piracy efforts by purchasing a copy of this book at the authorized online outlets.

Nelle L'Amour thanks you for your understanding and support.

To join my mailing list for new releases, sales, and giveaways, please sign up here:
NEWSLETTER: nellelamour.com/newsletter

NICHOLS CANYON PRESS
Los Angeles, CA USA

Cover by Arijana Karčić/CoverIt Designs
Proofreading by Virgina Tesi Carey
Formatting by BB eBooks

Dedicated to my fur baby Pepper, who gives me great joy every second of the day.
An in remembrance of Pokey, Luna, and Inky, who will live in my heart forever.

On my honor, I will do my best
To do my duty to God and my country and to obey the Scout Law;
To help other people at all times;
To keep myself physically strong, mentally awake, and morally straight.
—The Scout Oath

THAT MAN 8

Chapter 1
Jennifer

*C*lick.

"Blake, do you hear that?" I whispered, fear creeping into my bones. My heart pounded against my ribs. And my chest constricted.

Just home from our amazing trip to Scotland, in time for my twenty-sixth birthday, I'd tossed and turned for hours, unable to fall asleep. I was suffering from jet lag. I anxiously glanced at the clock on my nightstand—it was only ten p.m., but in Scotland, it was six o'clock in the morning. Almost time to wake up.

I heard another barely audible click. It sounded like it was coming from the door to our condo—like the deadbolt was unlocking. Someone was trying to break in! I was positive!

"Blake!" I repeated, my voice rising over his light snoring. He was sound asleep, his chest gently rising and falling. I swear my husband could sleep through a 9.0 earthquake unlike me, who was a light sleeper because of the deep-seated anxiety I still harbored.

Someone had tried to rape me when I was in college, and that someone—a deranged game show producer—had tried to kill me shortly after I joined Conquest Broadcasting and would have had Blake not shown up—just in the nick of time—and stopped him. Don Springer was out of my life for good and while I'd gone into therapy after the harrowing life and death experience and taken a self-defense course, I was still traumatized by the slightest disturbance.

"Blake, wake up!!" I said in my loudest hushed voice, nudging his shoulder.

He shifted in the bed, pulling the duvet up to his chin. "What's going on?" he murmured, his voice groggy and his eyes still glued shut.

"Listen! Do you hear that?" I repeated. The rattling sound was unmistakable. The front door had been opened. "Someone's in the house!" Panic in my voice, I bolted upright. A cold shudder skated down my spine.

Consciousness slowly filled Blake. His long-lashed eyelids fluttered, then blinked open. His irises glowed midnight blue in the darkness. Shoving the covers down, he pushed himself up to a sitting position.

Neither of us said another word. Light footsteps thudded in our ears, followed by the clatter of drawers and cabinets slamming open and shut. The frightening reality finally sank into my husband. Wearing not a stitch of clothing, he jumped out of bed. My eyes trained on his magnificently sculpted body—those gorgeous rock-hard glutes and long muscular legs—as he hurried to his walk-in closet.

"Blake, what are you doing?"

"Shh! Be quiet and stay still! I'm getting a weapon!"

A weapon? Given that we lived in a luxury, high-security doorman building, we didn't keep a gun in the apartment. Even after the incident at my former duplex. The closest thing we had was the set of butcher knives in the kitchen. And my pepper spray, which was likewise in the kitchen in my backpack. But those weren't going to help.

My heart beating double time, I watched as Blake flung the closet door open and re-emerged with a long stick in one hand, the other gripped around a small object I couldn't discern.

"What are you holding?"

"My Little League baseball bat!" He held it up, flexing his pronounced bicep as he brandished it, and then tossed me the small object. With a thump, it landed on the bed close to me.

"W-what's this?" I stammered, reaching for the small shiny object.

"My Swiss Army Boy Scout knife."

Under normal circumstances, I would have playfully challenged my husband's claim to being a Boy Scout—*Boy Scout's honor*—but this was hardly the time. Our lives were in danger.

"Hold on to it and call 911!" Gripping the bat, he tiptoed toward our bedroom door.

"Blake, I'm scared! Be careful!"

He disappeared. Without wasting a second, I grabbed my phone and called 911.

Chapter 2
Blake

My heart beat like a jackrabbit's as I stealthily crept down the dark hallway that led to the living room. Every nerve was on edge, every sense on high alert. More footsteps thudded in the near distance, followed by the clamor of dishes and silverware. We were definitely being robbed!

Breathing in and out of my nose, I gripped my bat tighter, willing myself to stay rational and in the moment. My mind swam with questions and worst-case scenarios. What if the burglar had a knife or a gun? What if he attacked me? Took me by surprise? And maybe there were two of them! More than anything, I hoped my tiger, whom I loved more than life itself—the woman I would slay dragons for—would be safe. Then, an unsettling afterthought hit me. Shit. I forgot to tell her to lock the bedroom door, but now it was too late. Naked as I was, I mentally donned my red cape. I was *That Man*, her superhero and protector.

In my head, I formed a plan of attack. The room

pitch black, I would sneak up on the perpetrator and before he had a chance to hear or see me, I'd bash him over the head with the bat . . . or take a swing at him if he dared to make a move on me. Either way, knock him out cold, kick in his balls for good measure, and then tie him up, waiting for the police to arrive. Fingers crossed they were already on the way and soon sirens would be wailing in my ears.

Armed with my bat and my plan, I tried to steady my shaky breaths as I stepped foot into the living room. Suddenly, the overhead lights flashed on. I blinked once and let out a startled scream.

And so did *she!*

Chapter 3
Blake

"Blakela! *Vhat* are you doing *vith* that baseball bat?"

"Grandma! What are *you* doing here?"

"*Vhat* does it look like? I'm making you and Jennifer a nice Shabbat dinner with the leftovers from your parents' house. *Vhat* are you doing home? Your father said you *veren't* landing until midnight."

As she continued to set the table in our dining alcove and dole out hefty portions of the brisket and kugel, I explained to her that Jen and I had managed to catch an earlier non-stop flight out of Edinburgh instead of our later one that connected in London.

"Travel *shmavel,*" she muttered, transferring the remaining brisket into a Tupperware container. "I've also got a beautiful challah and some delicious homemade matzo ball soup in my shopping bag. *Vant* me to heat it up?"

"No thanks, Grandma," I muttered, still doing a mental reset. "We'll have it tomorrow."

"Vhatever. Just don't let it go to *vaste."* She started putting the food away in the fridge. "So, how *vas* Scotland?"

"It was great," I replied, leaving out the details of our many sexcapades, including our kinky kilt sex.

"Kenahora! Did you make me some *kindela?"* Grandma was obsessed with Jen and me having a baby—and making her a great grandmother. She wasn't aware of the challenges we faced on account of Jen's partial hysterectomy.

Evading her question, I told her that we brought back kilts for both her and Luigi, her jovial second husband. My personal tailor, who added crotch room to my trousers. Go figure.

Dropping the sensitive subject to my great relief, she informed me that Luigi was waiting for her downstairs in their car. Then, her eyes roamed down my body, and I suddenly realized I was standing stark naked in front of my eighty-five-year-old grandmother! Mortification raced through me as words failed me.

"Bubula, you should put on some pajamas. Your *shmekel* is going to catch a cold!"

Hastily, I dashed to the sofa and grabbed the needlepoint pillow that Jen had bought me in Scotland and held it against my groin. I looked down at the words stitched into the canvas: *It ain't easy being king.* The words rang true.

"So *vhere's* Jennifer?" asked Grandma with a dramatic shrug, lifting her palms up.

On cue, Jennifer appeared, her eyes wide with shock until her face relaxed with a smile of relief. My Swiss Army knife in her hand, she was wearing a pair of my polka dot boxer shorts and a tight little T-shirt that I bought her in Scotland with the words: *It's Scot to be good.* Her perfectly pert petite tits grazed the thin cotton fabric. She looked adorable! And so fuckable! I was amazed by how fast I'd gone from murderous thoughts to lustful ones. My sexy wife could do that to me.

"Grandma! What are you doing here?" Sauntering toward us, she dropped her would-be assault weapon on our home bar.

I explained that Grandma had come over to deliver a Shabbat meal, not knowing we'd gotten home earlier than expected. Her eyes flitted to the dining table and her face brightened even more.

"Oh, Grandma, that's so thoughtful of you! Blake and I thought you were a burglar!"

"Burglar, *shmurglar!*" With a roll of her eyes, she dismissively flicked a hand. "Eat, *bubulas,* before everything gets cold!"

Just as we were about to sit down, a loud knock sounded at the door. *Rap, rap, rap, rap.*

"Police! Open up!"

Crap! I'd totally forgotten that I'd asked my tiger to call 911. In my naked state, I stood frozen as a statue, my feet super-glued to the floor.

"I'll get it," chirped Jen, already darting to the door. My eyes stayed on her as she swung it open. Three stern, armed cops, two men and a woman, stood at the threshold. A shiver ran down my spine at the sight of their weapons. And then my toes curled as their gaze raked over my naked body. I pressed the pillow tighter against Mr. Burns, as I affectionately called my cock, instinctively protecting him. A heart palpitating mix of fear and embarrassment swept over me.

"Is everything okay here?" asked the staunch female cop, her dark eagle eyes scanning the apartment before returning to me in my naked state. I felt myself flushing, heat crawling to my cheeks. Sheepishly, I wiggled the fingers of my free hand and waved hi.

"Yes, officer," chimed in Jen. "We thought we had an intruder, but it was just my husband's grandmother. We're so sorry for the inconvenience."

The three cops looked at each other, not letting their guard down.

"*Bubulas, vould* you like some brisket?" interjected Grandma, totally nonplussed. "There's more than enough for *everyvon!*"

The older male cop studied her. "You look familiar." Then, he rubbed his dimpled chin with a thumb. "Hey, aren't you on TV?"

Grandma explained she hosted *The Sexy Shmexy Book Club*. The ever-popular talk show Jen had developed.

The cop's face lit up. "Holy baloney! My wife loves that show!"

"Mine, too!" beamed the other male cop.

"Me too!" blurted the lady cop, adding that she'd read every single one of the books they'd discussed.

Five minutes later everything was back to normal. Grandma promised the three police officers signed books and invited them—and a guest—to one of her show tapings. And then, they all left, leaving Jen and me alone.

I let out a deep breath, tossing the pillow back on the couch. "Phew! I'm glad that's over! If you think about it, that was pretty funny."

Jen did not return my smile. "If you *really* think about it, it wasn't that funny! What if it had been a real burglar? And even worse, what if you hadn't been here?"

The thought of any harm coming to my tiger rattled me. She had a point. I traveled a lot for business, leaving her alone in the apartment. Often when I was away, her best friend Libby stayed over, but even though Libby was as tough as nails, she wouldn't stand a chance against a built-like-a-brick-house intruder—armed with a weapon no less. She was as vulnerable as my beloved tiger. Maybe I needed to hire a bodyguard to protect my wife when I went out of town. I made a mental note to have my secretary Mrs. Cho look into one before I was distracted by the scrumptious smell of Grandma's brisket. My stomach rumbled as my eyes panned to the set table.

"Hey, baby, we're up and I'm hungry. We might as well eat."

Jen agreed, and I was thankful she dropped the subject of a home invasion. While she went to fetch a bottle of red wine from our collection, I sat down at the table. Holding a bottle of Rutherford Cabernet and two wineglasses, she joined me and poured us each a glass.

After toasting each other, I turned the subject to our favorite sexy times in Scotland as we devoured the delicious brisket meal. The naughtiest had been an impromptu fuck on the canopied bed of Mary, Queen of Scots, when the castle guards weren't looking. Eating my tiger's pussy under her kilt at a local tavern came in a close, hot second. The conversation only made me hungrier. Hungry for my tiger. *Gantin* for her as the Scots would say. I was still naked as a jaybird and beneath the table, my cock stirred.

We left not a morsel on our plates, wiping them clean with chunks of the challah Grandma had also brought. My eyes stayed fixed on Jen as she stood up with her plate and utensils in hand. "Blake, hand me yours. I'll put everything in the dishwasher."

God, my high-powered wife was cute when she was in domestic mode. But she was even cuter when she was on the floor under me.

"Put everything down. It can wait. And besides, I'm still ravenous."

She set her plate back down on the table. "Do you want more? Should I heat up the soup?"

I silently chortled. Yeah, I wanted more, but not another slab of brisket. Or some fluffy dough balls. When it came to my wife, I had my own set of balls and a very hearty appetite. My cock twitched and a new little plan of attack formulated in my head.

"On second thought, baby, let's put things away and call it a night."

"Sure. That works for me. I'm beat!"

With a hidden smile, I placed my fork and knife on my plate, but as I was about to give them to her, the utensils "accidentally" fell onto the floor. I bent over to reach for them and then groaned, making a pained face.

"Aagh! My back! I think I pulled a muscle!"

Alarm filled my tiger's glittering emerald eyes as I silently snickered. I was such a good actor. Seriously, I deserved an award.

"Oh my God, Blake! Don't move! I'll pick them up." She leaped up from her seat and rounded the table to retrieve the utensils, squatting down just as I anticipated. Perfection! I sprung up from my chair, Mr. Burns springing up with me, and joined my wife on the floor, kneeling behind her.

"Blake! What are you doing?"

"Get down on your hands and knees," I ordered.

Obediently, without a word, she did as she was told, her gorgeous heart-shaped ass high in the air. Not wasting a second, I yanked down her boxer shorts and managed to slide them past her ankles. Then, I curled a finger under her, caressing her tender swells until they were all slick and wet.

"Oh God, Blake," she moaned as I moved my finger to her clit, rubbing it vigorously. She moaned again, arching her back like a stretching cat. She was ready. I was ready . . . to pummel *my* pussy from behind. Doggy style!

Planting my hands on the floor on either side of her narrow hips, I spread her legs and then wedged Mr. Burns inside her. My big, thick cock slid in with ease, taking her to the hilt, and then I began to pound her. Pumping in and out harder and faster as she met my thrusts.

More moans. Whimpers. Pants. And grunts on my part. It was an intense wordless fuck. Truthfully, most of them were like that. I'd read some of the steamy romance novels that Jen had made into movies and could never understand all the banter that transpired between the amorous couples during their most intimate times. Hell, I couldn't even think straight let alone get coherent words out. At most some garbled dirty talk. Three letter Boggle words limited to "hot," "wet," and "yes." A few expletives and then, "Come for me, tiger." Or, "Baby, I'm gonna come!"

And boy, was I. It was a little premature for me, but who knew what effect tonight's traumatic events and jet lag had on me. I was ready to let go. Explode!

With one more forceful thrust and a feral grunt, I emptied inside her, feeling my tiger's own explosive orgasm chasing mine. As she combusted around me, she roared out my name, so loudly the Highlanders we'd met in Scotland likely heard her.

I gripped her abdomen before she sank to the floor.

Still folded over, she exhaled a loud breath and then muttered:

"Blake, we need to get a dog."

Chapter 4
Blake

It was Saturday. Usually, I got up early to climb the Santa Monica stairs, but today I slept in. It was almost ten a.m., which was really late for me, and as I rolled out of bed, the alluring smell of fresh coffee wafted from the kitchen. Jen was already up and must have made it. The strong aroma brought me to my senses, and I remembered it was my wife's birthday. Her twenty-sixth. I had plans to make her day special. Make that very special. And those plans included a romp in the sack with Mr. Burns after I gave her the bauble I'd secretly bought in Scotland.

After doing my morning business, I joined her at the kitchen bar, which overlooked the living room and dining area. Seated on a counter stool, she was hunched over her laptop, a mug of coffee beside her.

"Happy Birthday, baby," I said cheerfully, before making myself a cup of coffee. The way I liked it—lots of cream and two sugars.

It was almost as if she didn't hear me. "Oh my God,

they're all so cute!" she gushed as I headed her way.

"What's so cute?" I gave her a kiss on the nape of her neck and then sat down next to her, carefully setting my hot coffee on the counter. She'd better not be referring to any hot looking guys!

"These doggies!" Her eyes glued to the screen, she scrolled down. "Take a look!" She angled the computer in my direction, myriad photos of dogs facing me on the screen. There were all different types, some small, some big, and a wide variety of breeds, ranging from purebreds to mutts.

Jen took a sip of her coffee. "Blake, I want all of them! And they all need good homes!"

Jen had mentioned that she wanted a dog after we fucked last night, but in all honesty, I hadn't thought much about it. I figured it was just a random thought, but I guess I was wrong.

I slid the laptop back her way. "What site are you on?"

"Adopt-a-Pet. There are literally hundreds of dogs you can adopt." She took another sip of her steamy brew. "Blake, did you ever have a dog growing up?"

I told her we'd had a half dozen. All of them yappy white miniature poodles that my socialite mother had flown in from a top East Coast breeder. Every one of them had a French name—Monique, Brigitte, Gigi—to name a few. My mother fawned over them, spoiling them with gourmet meals our cooks prepared, designer accessories and outfits she had custom-made in Paris, and canopied beds that were miniature copies of the regal one she and my father slept in. My father let her have her way with the dogs—even let her take them on vacations—as long as they didn't sleep in their bed. That's where he put his foot down.

Jennifer's face lit up. "Oh, Blake, they sound so adorable. I bet you must have loved them!"

I scrunched my brows, making a face. "Loathed them is more like it." Jen's brows shot up as I explained. "They were total pains in the ass. The spoiled brats peed all over the house and chewed up lots of shit, including my treasured baseball card collection. Plus, thanks to my sister being a bookworm and obsessed with getting into an Ivy-League college, I got saddled with the job of taking them for a walk after school. My father thought it was a great idea for his slacker son to have a responsible job and he even paid me five dollars per walk. Luckily, I figured out quickly that the gardener wanted the five bucks more than I did and secretly got him to give the dogs their daily afternoon walk.

I smiled at the memory of my achievement. Pass the buck was a life-lesson I taught myself. And it still worked.

Jen was not amused by my cleverness. Her face grew pensive, borderline worried. "Blake, does that mean you don't like dogs?"

I took a sip of my coffee. "No. It just means I'm not a dog person."

A glimmer of hope twinkled in her eyes. It was followed by a long beat of silence. She turned to face me, holding my gaze fiercely in hers.

"Blake, I was serious about what I said last night. I really want us to get a dog. Not a sappy little poodle, but one that can protect me when you're away. I'd feel so much safer that way."

"Baby, we don't need a dog. We live in a super-secure doorman building. We both work long hours and won't be able to walk it. Plus, we don't even have a yard!"

"But we have a terrace!"

She had a point. Her look of disappointment was getting to me. I had to appease her. "Why don't we wait until we buy a house, and then we can reconsider getting a dog." *Hahaha! We're NEVER getting a dog!*

Jen's eyes watered. She looked away from me, setting her eyes back on her computer screen and the photos of the rescue dogs. A tear escaped and fell onto her keyboard. Then another and another until she was a full-blown blubbering mess.

"All these poor adorable dogs with no homes! How could you feel that way, Blake?"

There was nothing that gutted me more than seeing my wife cry. I attempted to brush away her tears, but she wouldn't let me.

"Don't touch me!" The tears kept falling. We were having a fight. On *her* birthday, as she ruefully reminded me.

A half-hour later, we were pulling into the parking lot of the West LA Animal Shelter in my sparkling new black Porsche convertible.

Chapter 5
Jennifer

Unlike Blake, I'd never had a dog growing up. As much as I coveted one, being the sheltered, home-schooled, only child I was, it wasn't possible. My parents, as much as they loved me, refused to let me have one. I had a lot allergies (most of which I outgrew) and because they had me late in life, they were germaphobes and overprotective.

Finally, my lifelong dream of having a dog was about to come true. Or so I hoped. I had guarded optimism as Blake and I walked side by side through the animal shelter, led by a young, attractive volunteer named Tessa. My heart was breaking! God, there were so many dogs that needed good homes! And seeing their sad faces behind bars only made me feel worse.

"Can't we go any faster?" Blake's patience level was thin. He seemed disgruntled. Eager to leave. "Let's go out for a birthday brunch."

"But, baby, we just got here. There are so many more dogs to see."

I heard him grumble under his breath and reluctantly, he kept up with Tessa and me, dragging his feet behind him.

The shelter also housed other animals. Cats, bunnies, hamsters, and even a few birds. But most were dogs, the majority of them older pit bulls. Honestly, with their silky fawn gray coats and expressive light brown eyes, they were beautiful, but Blake had made it loud and clear that he didn't want one.

"It's imperative the dog we adopt is good with kids," he told Tessa.

At least that made me feel good. Our desire to have children was a challenging one on account of my partial hysterectomy, but my beloved husband hadn't lost hope. On that page, we were united.

"We'd also like a young dog, no older than a year," he added.

"Why?" I asked, thinking about all the needy older dogs that might face euthanasia. Though this place prided itself as a no kill shelter, it still had limitations as to how long a dog could remain.

"Because it'll live longer and be easier to train," he answered matter-of-factly. "You can't teach an old dog new tricks."

"That's not necessarily true," countered Tessa. "You'd be surprised by what an old dog can learn."

I sided with our guide but said nothing. At least Blake expressed an interest in engaging with our potential fur baby. Growing more and more impatient, he excused himself to use the men's room. I continued to walk up and down the aisles with Tessa, passing by all the dogs up for adoption.

My heart was getting heavier by the second, and the antiseptic smell of disinfectant combined with the cacophony of yelping dogs was making me queasy. No dog, no matter what the breed or age, belonged in a cage behind bars. Without a home. Without love. In my heart, I could hear each and every one of them crying out to me: Please take me home! Make me your forever fur baby! I felt tears verging as my pace slowed to a trudge.

"Are you okay, Jennifer?" asked Tessa, picking up on my growing gloom.

"Kind of. It just makes me feel so sad seeing all these poor abandoned dogs in cages." My gaze took in a particularly sad, overweight Bassett Hound, his ears as droopy as both his eyes and his gut. "How do you manage to hold it together? I don't think I could ever work here."

Reaching inside the pocket of the aqua smock she was wearing, she stopped in front of the cage. "Here, Bosco," she said, slipping a bone-shaped biscuit inside it. The dog immediately cheered up. Wagging his tail, he gobbled up the treat.

"Good boy!" My lovely dark-haired companion smiled. "It's not as hard as you think. We are a no kill shelter and 99% of our rescues find a good home. I live in a building that prohibits dogs so I derive a lot of joy spending time with them here. They are all so sweet, and I'm so happy I can give them love and attention until they find a new forever home. And it's a two-way street. They give me love back. This 'job' is so much more rewarding than my normal day job as a cashier—which I only do to make money. I'm trying to save up so I can one day go back to school and become a veterinarian."

Her words warmed my heart and I instantly felt better. "That's so awesome you want to become a vet. I hope your dream comes true."

At that moment, Blake returned. He looked constipated. Not one bit happy.

"Jen, we should go. We can come back and check out the dogs in a few weeks."

I felt his eagerness to leave in my bones, but I refused to oblige. I came here with a purpose, and that purpose was to go home with a dog. In my heart of hearts, I knew he—or she—was here waiting for me. I would recognize *my* dog when I saw it.

"Blake, you can go home, but I'm not leaving until I've seen all the dogs. I just know our fur baby is here."

"Fine." He hurled the word at me as Tessa led us to the last row of kennels.

And there he was! Inside the very last cage! Inky black, muscled, his expressive face glued to the bars. His big, beautiful chocolate brown eyes latched onto mine.

"Oh my goodness!" I gasped. "Who's this?"

"Scout," replied Tessa. "He just came in this morning."

"Really?"

"He's an eight-month-old Lab mix."

"Oh, he's just a baby!"

Tessa laughed. "A *big* baby! He weighs sixty pounds, but he shouldn't get too much bigger."

"What's his story?"

"He comes from a very nice family with two young kids."

"Blake, did you hear that? He's good with children!"

My love furrowed his brows, suspicion etched in the crease between them. "Why did they give him up?"

"The husband is being transferred to a country abroad that won't allow canine pets to be brought in. He's been well taken care of, neutered, micro-chipped, and is up to date on all his shots. I was also told he's housebroken."

He was sounding more and more perfect with each word. Plus with his sleek shorthaired coat, he'd likely not require a lot of grooming. Or shed much. Excitement surged inside me.

"Hi, Scout!" Our eyes stayed locked and then he began to wag his tail. Followed by a sweet whimper as if he was saying hi back, his big pink tongue lolling out of his mouth. It reminded me of the strawberry taffy my parents used to buy me whenever we went on vacation to Lake Michigan. Such sweet memories.

"Tessa, can I spend a little one-on-one time with him?"

"Of course." She bent down to unlock the ground-level kennel to let Scout out.

A few moments later, I was on my knees, hugging Scout as he licked my face. Oh God, this velvety, sixty-pound bundle of sweetness was giving me kisses! Delicious wet kisses! This was my dog! Our fur baby!

I knew it.

"Blake, I'm so in love with him! Please let's make him ours!"

My husband pinched his lips, then blew out a sharp, resigned breath from his nose. His nostrils flared.

"Fine. Let's fill out the paperwork."

A half-hour later we were back in Blake's Porsche. The top down. Scout squeezed next to me in the front seat. His head tilted back, his snout catching the wind, and enjoying every minute of the ride.

"Blake, this is the best birthday present ever!"

"Don't thank me." His voice flat, my husband kept his eyes on the road.

I didn't read too much into his words and instead hugged Scout, happiness soaring inside me.

"Scout, sweetie, I'm your new mommy!"

How wonderful it felt to say that word.

Mommy.

Chapter 6
Blake

Anyone who knew me knew I loved to shop. I was a veritable shopaholic. Heaven to me was visiting a beauty supply store and stocking up on every moisturizer known to mankind. And don't even get me started on going to the Westfield mall in Century City or walking down Rodeo Drive in Beverly Hills. I could spend hours in the Apple Store or Best Buy and walk out with all kinds of crap I didn't really need, and drop an easy fifty grand on a half-dozen new custom-made Brioni suits and matching accessories.

But, let me tell you, shopping at Petco was not my idea of heaven. It was more like hell. Jen had insisted we stop at the one in Westwood before we drove home to pick up a few things for Scout. Reluctantly, I agreed, thinking we'd be in and out quickly. To pick up a bag of kibble and some bowls for his food and water. Boy, was I wrong!

We'd already been in the pet emporium for over an hour. I was charged with walking Scout on the leash the shelter had given us as we strolled down the aisles, Jen pushing a large red shopping cart, me trying to hold the dog back every time he saw a fellow canine. I wasn't sure if he wanted to play with them or attack them. All I knew was that the sixty-pound beast was strong as an ox, and despite what good shape I was in, it took all my effort to hold him back. Worry gnawed at me. God knows what damage he could cause if he got loose. From tearing up the store to tearing off someone's leg. My mother always said there's no such thing as a bad dog, but I knew this was not true. Just think about Cujo! Need I say more?

My wife was not the shopaholic I was, but I swear she was like a kid in a candy store, grabbing everything in sight. Our cart was filled to the gill, the items including two twenty-pound bags of kibble, several giant bottles of puppy vitamins, a variety of treats (Jen wanted to experiment), a large dog bed, an even larger pillow he could rest on, a red felt dog coat in case the weather grew cold or we took him with us to Sun Valley (fat chance!), plus a gazillion toys, ranging from squeaky plush ones to exercise balls.

The cart must have weighed a ton, and I saw that my petite tiger was straining to push it.

"Jen, why don't I push the cart and you hold Scout?" She might as well get used to it because there was no way in hell I was going to walk this animal. And with me in charge of the cart, the faster we could get out of here. My tiger agreed and I was shocked by how nicely Scout walked with her.

"Blake, there's just one more thing we need."

Seriously? Like a hole in the head?

"We should get Scout a new collar and leash. His look kind of worn out."

I glanced down at the ones he was wearing. Truthfully, they were rather hideous . . . synthetic, all chewed up in a grungy, faded shade of blue. Plus, they were likely filled with germs. The germaphobe I was, I made a mental note to apply some hand sanitizer as soon as we got out of this joint. Fortunately, I kept some Purell in my glove box.

As luck would have it, we were by the collars and leash section, the matching sets hanging on several racks. The collars hooked, the leashes dangling, ranging in size to accommodate the smallest dog to the largest one. By the size of Scout's neck, he was somewhere in the middle.

"What about this red leather collar?" I said, pointing to it. It looked simple and sturdy. There was no way I was going to have this dog wear some frou-frou collar with rhinestones like those my mother's poodles wore.

Jen smiled. "I like it. Do you think it'll fit him?"

"Try it on for size."

Slipping it off the rack, Jen bent down and put it around Scout's neck. I was surprised by how submissive he was with her. He sat patiently as she buckled it and wagged his tail like a metronome.

"It fits great, Blake." She tucked her hand inside it. "And there's even enough room in case he grows." Scout lifted his head and made goo-goo eyes with my wife, giving her the goofiest look I'd ever seen. His mouth parted wide, his tongue dangling. With a smile that could light up the sky, Jen cupped his jaw and planted a loud kiss on the top of his head.

I bristled. *What about me? Don't I get a kiss? Hello! I'm your husband and the schmuck who schlepped here.*

"Baby boy, you look so handsome in your new collar!"

Baby boy? So handsome? Give me a frigging break!

Jen's eyes darted back to the rack of collars and leashes. "Which type of leash should we get?"

There were two different types. The retractable kind and the regular kind. I opted for the latter, thinking my wife would have more control over it. There was no doubt in my mind that Calamity Jen, as her best friend Libby aptly called her, would get all tangled up in the long retractable leash, trip, get dragged a mile, and end up in the emergency room. Not wanting that to happen, I told her to get the six-foot leather one that matched the collar.

"Are we done?" I asked as she attached the leash to Scout's new red collar, leaving the price tags on.

Unfazed by my blatantly irritated tone, Jen surveyed

the piled up cart. "Yup, I think so. On the way out we'll get him a new name tag with one of our phone numbers inscribed on it."

An evil thought crossed my mind. Maybe I'd offer to do that while she was at the check out counter and "accidentally" forget to include a phone number or screw up a digit so this beast couldn't be traced back to us if he ran away. Unfortunately, Jen beat me to it, leaving me to unload the cart and swipe my credit card. The bill came to over five hundred dollars . . . and that wasn't counting his new leather collar and leash, which would likely add another hundred bucks. Jen returned quickly, with Scout proudly wearing his new red bone-shaped identification tag.

"All done," she beamed, as the cashier added in the cost of the collar and leash and then bagged all the items, except the dog bed, pillow, and kibble.

"Good." As I snatched the receipt from the cashier, I felt a warm liquid saturating my jeans and sneakers. Bristling, I lowered my eyes and I swear I wanted to toss the beast out the door. Or wring his neck, new collar and all. The goddamn dog had peed on me!

"Fuck!" I couldn't contain myself.

"We're sorry," murmured Jen, apologizing more to the cashier than to pee-soaked me. In addition to drenching my new Diesel jeans and twelve hundred dollar Air Jordans, the dog had left a golden puddle around my feet.

The nose-pierced cashier laughed. "No need to apologize. It happens all the time."

My blood bubbled as Shelter Girl's words whirled in my head. *And I was also told he's housebroken.*

A new unsettling thought zipped into my head. What if he wasn't?

The thought didn't last long. There was a new pressing problem. How the hell were we going to fit all this shit into my two-seater car? Plus Jen and the goddamn dog?

Thankfully, I learned from the cashier that Petco had just launched a delivery service, free to anyone who spent more than twenty-five dollars. I'd gladly pay them anything they demanded to deliver the dog too.

To anyone's place other than mine.

The further away the better.

Chapter 7
Blake

An excited Scout gallivanted through our two-bedroom apartment. Going from room to room, sniffing everything. He even checked out the terrace.

"Aww, Blake! He's so cute, making himself at home," cooed Jen, hanging his leash around the front door handle. "I wish Petco would get here already. I bet he's hungry and I'm so eager to get everything set up."

"I'm sure they'll be here any minute." We'd told the doorman to let him up. He'd likely need to borrow a dolly with all the stuff we'd bought. Then, a moment later the doorbell rang.

Ding-dong. Ding-dong.

At the sound, Scout went berserk. Running around the living room in circles. Then barking at the door like crazy! Growling! Snarling! Bearing his large, canine fangs!

Ding-dong. Ding-dong.

Foaming at the mouth, the dog was a total nutjob! He'd turned into Cujo! Just as I'd feared.

Jennifer beamed. "Blake, he's such a good guard dog! I'm so pleased!"

"How are we going to open the door?" I asked, having to shout over Scout's loud, incessant yelps. "What if he attacks the delivery guy?"

My inner voice screamed lawsuit. The bell chimed again followed by several loud raps on the door. The beast grew more incensed, more vicious, but my tiger remained cool as a cucumber.

"Blake, hold him back by his collar."

"But, Jen, what if he bites off my hand?"

"He won't. He knows and trusts you."

The problem was I didn't trust him. Not one iota. "Why don't we just have the Petco guy leave the stuff with the concierge and I'll bring it up." *Or get someone to do it.*

"Blake, that's ridiculous! Just hold Scout back and I'll put his leash on him."

Reluctantly, my nerves buzzing like a swarm of bees, I hooked my right hand under Scout's collar and as I gripped it, Jen clipped on the leash. With all the muscle power I could muster, I yanked Scout away from the door, holding him in place. He was still in attack mode, a runway of hair bristling on his back.

Jen opened the door. A gangly, pimple-faced kid, who looked to be no more than eighteen, stood at the entrance with a dolly piled up with all the pet supplies we'd bought. He immediately caught sight of I'm-gonna-have-you-for-lunch Scout, who was still growling and barking like mad. Terror filled the whites of his eyes, his body stiffening. Using both hands, I held Scout back, putting him on a tight leash.

"Um, uh, do you want me to bring everything in?" the kid asked nervously.

"If you could just push the dolly inside, I'd really appreciate it." The pimply kid quickly did as he was asked and after Jen gave him a tip, he scurried off like his butt was about to be lit.

Thank the canine gods, Scout calmed down. I took off his leash and watched with Jen as he loped up to the dolly, sniffing the giant bags of kibble.

"Blake, he's definitely hungry."

"Yeah." *Especially since he didn't get the opportunity to eat the delivery kid and suck the pus out of his pimples*, I silently added, before offering to hump one of the twenty-pound bags into the kitchen. Scout followed me, along with my tiger, carrying his food and water bowls.

I ripped open the bag of dog food and using a scooper we already had, Jen filled up one of the large bowls. Scout made a beeline for the dog chow, scarfing it down. Every single morsel.

"Wow, Blake! Our poor baby was so hungry!"

I'd never seen a dog gobble up his food so quickly. Jen fetched him some water while I watched him clean his bowl. Thank goodness, he liked kibble, unlike my mother's prissy poodles, and we didn't have to prepare him homemade meals. Score one point for him, but I still wasn't convinced this dog was a good idea.

Jen filled up his water bowl and set it beside him. He took several noisy slurps. Things seemed under control.

"Jen, I'm going to go out and do the stairs and when I come back, we'll put everything away."

"I have a better idea!" She bent down and affectionately stroked Scout's slick, shiny head. "Baby boy, do you want to go out for a walk with your daddy?"

The dog happily let out a woof as Jen offered to put everything away.

Fuck me.

And fuck this Daddy shit.

Chapter 8
Blake

I took Scout to Santa Monica's Palisades Park. The verdant stretch had a popular mile-long pedestrian path overlooking the Pacific Ocean that started at San Vincente, not far from the steps, and ended at the Santa Monica Pier. I knew it was dog friendly as I'd seen other dog walkers there before. Dogs, however, were not allowed to run free and had to be contained on a leash.

So far so good. The car ride had gone well, with Scout again behaving in the now towel-covered front seat, the top down. He even seemed to enjoy the music I played, running the gamut from Smokey Robinson to The Chainsmokers. He'd, however, better not get too used to my car; it was my favorite toy (not counting the deluxe five-speed vibrator I'd given Jen for Christmas) and had cost a fortune. I treated it like a baby. One bad move on the mongrel's part and he might be dog chow.

The mid October air was SoCal mild and the sun was shining brightly. It was a beautiful day and as I briskly walked Scout down the grassy path, I took in things I generally didn't observe when I was jogging or doing the steps. Below, the majestic white crested waves... the surfers... the wide sandy white beach... kids frolicking. Around me, artists painting at easels... parents picnicking with their children... tufts of flowers surrounding the tall palm trees... well-toned bodies practicing yoga... and sadly, the many homeless people camping out on the grass. Fortunately, Scout seemed unfazed by the latter, more interested in finding a good spot to pee. Or to take a dump.

"Good boy," I commended as he lifted his long hind leg, ten minutes into our walk. One bowel movement to go and we could head back to the car, which I'd parked in a metered spot along Ocean Avenue. Along the way, many fellow pedestrians and dog walkers told me what a good-looking dog he was. I must admit I was a little taken back, their praises going to my head. Yup, Scout was a stud like me. And for the first time I noticed, how well endowed he was. He was built like a horse. And honestly could be a porn star. Being in the business, I'd heard of dogs fucking their mistresses. There was even a crazy producer who'd once pitched me a series called *Fucking Lucky*. It was about a bored suburban housewife, who got off on doing it with her dog, Lucky. Bestiality was not my thing. Needless to say, I passed on the idea and told him with a straight face to pitch it to Animal Planet.

Halfway down the promenade, a little Latino girl, accompanied by her mother, asked me if she could pet Scout. *Por favor.*

"Yeah, sure," I replied. I regretted my words as soon as I said them. Despite Shelter Girl insinuating that Scout was good with kids, I wasn't sure. I had no proof. Shit! What if he bit the kid?

As the child's hand set down upon his slick back, Scout jerked away. Almost yanking my arm out of its socket and forcing the leash out of my hand. Before I could blink, he was charging down the path like a runaway train. Chasing after a stupid squirrel.

"Fuck!" I yelled. The girl's mother fired me a dirty look and started to curse in Spanish.

Not excusing myself, I took off after Scout. I swear he was a freaking super dog, running at hell-bent speed, his paws barely touching the ground. Trying to catch up with him, I ran faster, my lungs and limbs burning, my breath coming out in short, heated pants. Everything was a blur and I almost knocked some people over in my hot pursuit. My thoughts wavered between losing this dog for good and disappointing my tiger forever. Though the scale was tipped heavily in favor of the former, guess what thought won?

Yup, retrieving him. I couldn't bear the thought of my wife mourning her loss. Especially on her birthday. She seemed to love this beast as much as I loved her.

"Scout," I shouted at the top of my lungs. "Stop!

Come back!"

Maybe the family who previously owned him spoke Spanish or Korean or some other language, but he sure as hell didn't seem to understand English. Panic flooded me as he neared the always-crowded Santa Monica Pier. Home of Pacific Park, a world famous amusement park. The spinning Ferris wheel and whipping rollercoaster filled my vision. On my next blink, I lost sight of the scoundrel.

Breathless and frantic, I dashed off the walkway as it came to an end and hurried onto the Pier. With the glorious weather and it being a Saturday, the boardwalk was dense with visitors of all ethnic backgrounds and ages. My heart was palpitating and I was sweating like a pig. I bent over for a few seconds, hugging my thighs and catching my breath. Then straightening, I spun around like the carousel, my eyes darting in every direction. He was nowhere in sight. Dammit. The crazy mutt could be anywhere! At a fast food stand! Waiting in line for a ride! Maybe on a ride! Or he'd bolted down the adjacent Venice Boardwalk. And even worse, jumped off the wharf and gone for a swim in the ocean which was about fifty-feet below and only separated by a narrow railing. I knew a little bit about Labs, and they loved to swim. But me diving into the chilly ocean to retrieve him was not a likelihood. Maybe I should just let him swim out to sea, and he'd be picked up by some nice fisherman.

Who was I kidding? I needed to find this frigging dog and get him back home. Jen would be devastated if I told her he ran away. The birthday from hell. And she might hate me forever. Taking one more deep breath, I persevered and raced down the Pier, bumping into pedestrians and dodging kids in strollers, my eyes shifting left and right in hopes of finding him.

Heaving, I was breathless, my heart sinking faster than the Titanic. Where the hell could he be? A debilitating mixture of hopelessness and despair poured through my veins. What was I thinking to have adopted a young, crazy dog? *You can't teach an old dog new tricks.* You can't teach a dead one any. If we'd adopted an older, on-his-way-to-dog-heaven one, I might have been spared this insanity. After his demise and a brief mourning period, my life and Jen's would be back to what it was. Normal.

Stopping for a moment to collect myself, I blinked once. Twice. Then spotted him! Oh Jesus, how was I going to handle this?

Steadying my breathing, I jogged up to the brawny man in uniform. He was holding Scout tight on his leash. "Hi, officer, um, uh, that's my dog."

Scout didn't acknowledge me as the middle-aged cop shot me a stern look. "You're lucky the City of Santa Monica allows dogs on the Pier, but they have to be on a leash. There's a two hundred dollar fine for having a dog off leash. Can you read the sign?" He pointed to it.

Yeah, I can read, asshat! "I'm really sorry, *officer*," I mumbled in my most humble voice. "As you can see, I had him on his leash, but he bolted from me. He's a rescue; my wife and I just adopted him this morning. This is his first walk."

The cop's face lightened up. "Me and the missus have adopted many strays over the years." He handed me the leash, and I grabbed it as he continued. "I'm not going to write you up this time, but here's a word from the wise. Get him into training. The next time this happens you may not be so lucky and he'll end up back at the pound. And the fine will be double."

I profusely thanked the officer and told him I'd make a contribution to both the Policeman's Fund and our local pound.

To my great relief, Scout walked back calmly with me to my car, but I gripped his leash tightly, not taking any chances. Almost there, he stopped for a moment, squatting down. I watched him as he took the biggest dump ever. This was nothing like the little turds my mother's toy poodles left behind. It was giant and steaming. A flaming torpedo. Reluctantly, I picked up the stinky, hot deposit with the plastic bag I'd brought along and tossed it into the nearest trash receptacle. My eyes caught sight of a nearby sign. *Please pick up after your dog. Violators subject to a five hundred dollar fine.*

You're fucking welcome. I sneered.

We arrived at my car. Waiting for me was another stinkin' surprise.

A fricking ticket. Plastered under my windshield wiper. God knows how much it was going to cost for going over the one-hour only parking limit. And just by a lousy five minutes.

I cursed.

Life with this beast wasn't going to be easy.

Chapter 9
Blake

Jen was seated cross-legged on the couch when I returned with Scout, her MacBook on her lap. I managed to take off Scout's leash and hang it around the door handle before he went barreling into the living room to greet her.

A megawatt smile bloomed on my tiger's face as he sat down on the floor beside her. She affectionately stroked his head as he adoringly looked up at her with those deceptive big brown puppy eyes.

"Were you a good boy for Daddy?"

I felt every aching muscle in my body bunch up as I lumbered over to the bar to pour myself a shot of Scotch. I rarely drank so early in the day. Make that never. I knocked back the drink in a single gulp and poured myself another. This damn dog was driving me to drink! By this evening, I could be a raging alcoholic.

With my shot glass in hand, I joined Jen, plopping down onto one of the oversized chairs flanking the couch. Taking another chug of my drink, I stretched my long, crampy legs on the coffee table. Though I regularly did the challenging Santa Monica steps and worked out at my gym, this out of control dog had worn me out.

Wearing her glasses, Jen finally turned her attention to me. *Your adoring husband, remember?* "So, how did he do on his first walk?"

He was a total nightmare! The dog from hell! The holy terror ran away and I had to chase after him like a madman on the Pier. He cost me a parking ticket and almost gave me a heart attack.

I took another long swig of my drink. The alcohol burned my throat and was doing little to relax me. I felt my jaw clench as I lied through my teeth. "He was awesome! He did a nice pee and a big poop."

Jen's smile widened. She bent down and kissed Scout's head, showering him with praise and love. "What a good boy, Scout! I'm so proud of you!"

I gulped down more of my Scotch. *If you only knew!* Holding my tongue back, I switched the subject. "So what have you been up to?"

"I put all of Scout's things away. All his food is in the pantry and his toys are in a basket." She pointed to the large wicker basket in the corner. Close by was the large dog pillow we'd purchased.

"Where's his bed?"

"In our room. Next to ours. Being separated from his first family, he shouldn't sleep alone his first night here."

Silently, I bristled. That was way too close for comfort. He sure as hell better not come into our bed. And mind his own business when we fucked each other senseless. Tonight was going to be his first test. And possibly the beginning of two new commands: OFF! And GET LOST! I made a mental note to download the Google Translator app and find out how to say these words in a variety of languages in case the stupid dog didn't understand English. In the worst-case scenario, there was always a loud and clear NO! Every living thing understood that word, right?

Jen cut my mental ramblings short. "And Blake, while you were gone, I did a lot of research on Black Labs. They're super-loving and loyal, make great family pets, and are very intelligent. Oh, and they're also very rambunctious and need a lot of exercise."

Yeah, this one needs to run a marathon. A one-way trip to Hell! "Did any of the articles you read talk about obedience?"

Jen nodded. "Yes. They're easy to train because they're so smart."

I had a feeling this one was as stupid as stupid could be. It must be those unknown "mixed" genes that were bringing his IQ down by intervals. With his gangly body, long skinny tail, and narrow muzzle, he was far from being a pure pedigree Lab.

"And look what else I found online!" Excitement filled her voice and her face lit up as she flipped her computer around to face me.

"A SpongeBob doggie raincoat with a matching leash and collar! And even booties!!"

"Nice," I mumbled, staring at a shaggy dog that was dressed in the ridiculous bright-yellow ensemble. My wife was SpongeBob obsessed.

"I hope you don't mind that I ordered the whole set. From Chewy.com. It's such a great site." She cradled Scout's muzzle. "Oh baby boy, you're going to look so cute in your rain outfit!"

Yeah, and I just can't wait to walk you in the pouring rain and chase after you in the bloody mud. My tiger was too focused on Scout to notice the scowl on my face. I chugged the rest of my drink. Two down. I'd better stop before I got smashed.

"So, birthday girl, what do you want to do this afternoon?" We had plans to go out for dinner to celebrate with her best friends, Libby, Chaz, and Jeffrey, but I was hoping we could get a nice birthday fuck in before then. In addition to the bauble, I'd bought my tiger a new sex toy and I was eager to play with it.

"I think we should stay in and hang out with Scout. We can start teaching him some basic commands. You know like . . . sit, stay, and come."

The only living creature I wanted to order to come was my wife. That clearly wasn't happening. Damn this dog!

I mentally growled.

Chapter 10
Jennifer

"Blake, maybe we should cancel the dinner," I said as I shrugged on my slinky black dress. It was one of Chaz's designer samples—something he bestowed upon me often. "We can do it another time. I'm worried about leaving Scout alone on his first night here."

My husband was sitting on the edge of the bed, slipping on his Italian leather loafers. Sockless as usual. He looked sexy as sin in his casually elegant Brioni sports coat, crisp, open-collar white shirt, and a pair of ridiculously expensive designer jeans.

"Jen, baby, relax. He's going to be fine. He's done well so far. I think he likes it here."

I reflected on his words. They seemed rushed. Like he was eager to leave. Yet truthfully, Scout had done well. He had mastered a few commands—well at least, when I said them—and he was happy with all his toys. Right now as we got ready for my birthday celebration, he was resting in the living room on the large pillow we'd bought him, after having eaten his dinner and taken an evening walk. He seemed worn out from today's events. I couldn't blame him; so many adjustments! The poor baby!

"Blake, are you sure?" Uncertainty laced my voice.

"One hundred percent positive." My husband stood up as I struggled with the back zipper of my dress. "Let me help you."

As I studied myself in our full-length armoire mirror, I could see him swagger up to me. His eyes hooded, that cocky smirk curled on his gorgeous face.

A few heartbeats later, he was perched right behind me and I watched as he wrapped his arms around my waist and blew a hot breath on the back of my neck. I was wearing my contact lenses though Blake preferred me to wear my tortoiseshell eyeglasses, no matter what the occasion. They turned him on. He kissed me again.

"How do I look?" I managed as he fluttered butterfly kisses across my shoulders.

"Mmm. Very fuckable."

The hairs on the nape of my neck stood up and goosebumps popped along my bare arms. A blissful moan escaped as his warm hands sailed down my spine and reached my bottom. He squeezed my cheeks in his palms, his hard length pressed against me.

"God, baby! I so want to fuck you. Any way I can."

Then I let out a yelp as he slid a finger into my freshly showered backdoor entrance. His long, deft finger began to pump into me. Driving me to ecstasy.

My back arched and I met his finger thrusts, squeezing my muscles around his digit, longing to come. The thrusts came harder and faster, and I felt myself fall apart. And sag against him.

"Happy Birthday, tiger," Blake breathed into my ear as he withdrew his finger and slowly slid up the zipper. The metallic hiss sent another round of goosebumps to my skin. After another kiss on my neck, he took my hand. "C'mon. Let's go."

"Wait one sec," I said as Blake led me into the living room. He shot me a puzzled look as I broke free of his grip.

Balancing on my heels, I bent down and kissed Scout who was curled up sound asleep. "Don't worry, baby boy, we'll be back soon! Be a good boy for Mommy and Daddy."

CATCH was one of the hottest restaurants in LA. It took months to get a reservation there, but Chaz and his fiancé Jeffrey with all their connections had managed to score one. We were seated at a prime table in the breathtaking main dining room, feasting on jumbo shrimp and truffle sashimi and drinking Dom Pérignon. I hadn't seen them—or Chaz's twin sister Libby, my BFF—since our weeklong trip to Scotland. The conversation was lively, with my two dear gay friends wanting to know everything.

I zipped out my cell phone from my purse and showed them photos of our trip. Many of them were of Blake and me wearing our matching kilts.

"Oooh, Blakey, you look so cute in a skirt!" cooed Chaz.

"Nice legs," added Libby with a snicker.

"What did you wear underneath?" asked Jeffrey.

My husband blushed with embarrassment. The truth is, he went commando! And we fucked like Scottish bunnies. Sparing him from responding, I reached under the table and retrieved three small shopping bags.

"We brought you guys back presents." I handed each of my friends a bag and they simultaneously reached inside them. Whoots and thank yous all around. Each of them had gotten a beautiful tartan wool scarf, which we'd purchased at a charming shop in Edinburgh. While they likely wouldn't get much use in Los Angeles, my trio of friends traveled regularly for business to colder climates throughout the year. And would appreciate them.

"So, what did Blake get *you* for your birthday?" asked a tipsy Libby, with her scarf draped around her neck and guzzling her second glass of champagne. Libby had a tendency to drink a lot and become loose-lipped.

"This!" Picking up my phone again, I scrolled

through my photos until an adorable picture of Scout popped onto the screen. I'd taken a ton of photos of him in the afternoon, including selfies of the two of us, after he'd mastered the sit and stay commands. I handed the phone to Libby, who shared it with Chaz and Jeffrey, seated on either side of her. As they scrolled through the pics, they squealed, their rapid-fire comments overlapping.

"Oh my God! You got a dog!"

"He's so cute!"

"Where did you get him?"

"The West LA Animal Shelter."

"What's his name?"

"Scout."

"Like in Boy Scout?" asked Libby.

"Yes!" I winked at my husband. "Now, I have a *real* Boy Scout, right Blake?"

"Yeah, right." His voice flat, my husband did not seem amused by my little pun. He constantly told me he had once been a Boy Scout. *Scout's honor.* But he could never prove it and hence I didn't believe him.

A waiter came by and took our entrée orders. And not before long, we were feasting on a spread of delicious small-plated main dishes, ranging from Maryland crab cakes to New Zealand green mussels, plus a whole, grilled wild-caught branzino that we shared. Libby took it upon herself to order a second bottle of champagne, followed by a third one, and we all indulged. As to be expected, Chaz insisted we play a game. It was our ritual.

"Not truth or dare!" I begged, not wanting to play the blindfolded kissing game that had brought Blake and me together.

"No, but it does require a blindfold. These fabulous scarves will be perfect!"

Two minutes later I, the birthday girl, had Chaz's new plaid scarf wrapped around my eyes and my wrists bound behind my back with Jeffrey's. I was standing up and couldn't see or touch a thing. The game was called Sit 'n Snort, and it was simple. After being spun around a few times, I had to walk around the table and then sit on someone. Except before I started circling, my companions would exchange seats (or not) and place their chair cushions on their laps. It was my job to sit on one of their laps and when I did, they would snort, and I'd have to guess whose lap I was sitting on. Easy peasy, right? Wrong!

I was already feeling lightheaded from the champagne, and being the spaz I was, I almost tripped a few times. Moreover, everyone was already snorting like pigs, which made it hard not to laugh and tumble over. The sooner I sat on someone's lap the better. After a few more awkward, blindfolded steps, I gingerly lowered myself onto a cushion, hoping I wouldn't land on the floor on my butt.

A single snort. Hmm. Who could it be? I honestly

couldn't tell if it was one of the guys or Libby. *Snort, snort* again. Then, I felt a pair of strong knees bounce me.

Blake! I knew it and shouted out his name. On my next breath, the scarf around my eyes was swept off and before I could blink them open, a fierce passionate kiss smacked my lips. Oh, *That Man!*

Whoots from my friends filled my ears.

"Jenny-Poo! You won!" shouted Chaz. "Now, it's Blake's turn."

To be honest, I'd had enough of this silly game—I'd gotten my "prize"—and was eager to get home to check on Scout. Fingers crossed he was okay.

Then suddenly without warning, a harmonic rendition of "Happy Birthday" played in my ears. Still sitting on Blake's lap, I glimpsed a group of singing waiters coming our way with a lit up birthday cake. They set the cake down on the table in front of me.

"Close your eyes and make a wish, baby," urged Blake.

His arms wrapped around my waist, I did as he asked and blew out all the candles in a single breath.

There was only one thing I could wish for.

A baby.

Chapter 11
Blake

Holding a giant shopping bag filled with my tiger's presents—a new cocktail dress from Chaz, an elegant silver picture frame from Jeffrey that she planned to use for a Scout photo, and the board game Sexopoly, a gag gift from Libby,—I was about to unlock the door to our condo. Jen's best presents were yet to come. First, my own version of Sexopoly. This greedy bastard was going to *own* every inch of her being. Every heartbeat. Every breath. Every cell. Every bit of prime real estate. Her lips. Her tits. Her clit. Her pussy. I was going to fuck her into tomorrow. My cock flexed beneath my jeans as I inserted the key into the hole. I chuckled silently. A poetic metaphor.

"Blake, don't you think it's weird that Scout's not barking or scratching at the door?" asked Jen as I fumbled with the double lock. The stupid lock had always been a pain in the ass, and being somewhat plastered didn't help.

"Nah. He had a big day. I bet he's outside on the

terrace taking a snooze."

"That's not possible. I kept the sliding doors to the terrace locked. We need to dog-proof it before we can let him go outside by himself."

For a second, the image of him leaping off the terrace like Krypto the Superdog flashed in my head. It instantly faded as the safety bolt unlocked. Cranking the handle, I kicked the door open with my foot and we stepped inside the condo. The shopping bag dropped to the floor as my eyes almost popped out of their sockets.

"Holy fucking shit!"

"Oh my God!" shrieked Jen.

We'd stepped into a full-on blizzard in our living room.

No, not snowflakes, but a flurry of snow-white feathers swirling in the air everywhere. Scout had destroyed every one of our down-filled pillows, the tattered remnants scattered on the floor. Including the one Jen had bought me in Scotland with the words: *It ain't easy being king.*

Rage surged inside me. I was not going to let this dog royally screw with me. It was time to show him once and for all who was—make that *is*—king of this house. Who was the alpha. Swiping at the feathers, I scoured the room, looking for the bastard. Where the hell was he? Calling out his name several times, I looked left; I looked right. He was nowhere in sight. My hands clenched by my sides, I stormed out of the living room and marched toward our bedroom, my tiger trailing close behind me.

The bedroom was even a bigger disaster area than the living room. A total whiteout! All six pillows on our bed had been obliterated along with the goose down comforter. We were in a war zone!

"I'm going to teach that dog a lesson he'll never forget!"

Jen reached for my elbow, holding me back.

"Blake, please. Don't hurt him. He's only a puppy!" A mixture of desperation and fear laced her voice. She knew my adrenaline rivaled my testosterone. I was on a mission and nothing—I repeat NOTHING—was going to stop me.

You can run, but you can't hide, I gritted silently, clenching my teeth. Narrowing, my eyes circled the room as the endless feathers bombarded me. Almost blinding me. The beast was still nowhere in sight.

"I'll check your office and the guest bathroom," offered Jen, skirting off and leaving me alone.

I checked under the bed. Inside the walk-in closets. Behind the curtains. No Scout.

After checking our ensuite bathroom with no luck, I returned to the bedroom, surveying the mess. All my *après* dinner plans were in ruins. The king-size bed was no longer fit for a king, let alone a pauper. I'd conjured coming home to an epic session of making love with her new toy and then after a few orgasms, surprising her with the bauble I'd bought in Scotland. Before we went out, I'd hidden it under her stuffed white tiger. A gift to my wife on our first Christmas together, the plush animal was a permanent fixture on our bed. A symbol of our love. Surrounding it, every down-filled pillow was in shambles. The cases torn, the feathers leaking out. Limp as ragdoll sacks. But to my amazement, the tiger was intact, except for having fallen over. A sliver of relief sliced through my rage as I picked it up. The dainty little box was there, but not as I left it. The lid was off, pitted with teeth marks and missing the decorative stick-on bow. The velvet cushion inside the box was gone too, replaced by a bed of tiny feathers. Panicky, I picked up the ravaged box and shook it upside down, emptying the handful of feathers. Nothing was inside! I repeat: NOTHING. The bauble was gone! G-O-N-E. GONE!

My heart almost stopped, then it began to gallop. It had to be here! It had to! I flung all the deflated pillows along with the saggy comforter on the floor and searched the bed. Blindly feeling for a small metal object. Patting every inch of the mattress pad. Fuck. It wasn't here. Hopping off the mattress, I dropped to my knees and frantically began to crawl on the floor. Looking under the bed, turning everything upside down, shaking out shoes, and digging through the blanket of feathers. Nothing. Fucking nada unless you counted a dead spider. In a nano second, my focus went from where was the dog to where was my bauble. My throat constricted, my chest clenched.

And then Jen's voice resonated in my ears. "Blake, I found him! He was hiding in the guest bathroom and is fine."

Whoot for the fricking dog. I was the last thing from fine.

"Jen, leave him there and close the bathroom door. I need you!" Desperation filled my every word.

Sensing my urgency, Jen dashed into our bedroom. "Blake, what's wrong?"

Rising to my feet, I loped over to the bed and held up the box. "This!"

"It's just an old chewed up box."

"No, Jen. It's not just any old box. Your birthday present was inside it and now it's gone! I can't find it anywhere!"

"Scout must have hidden it. It's got to be somewhere."

"Well, trust me, it's not in this room! I've searched everywhere."

"Let me help." She brushed some feathers off her shoulders. "What should I be looking for?"

"A small platinum and diamond broach. A unicorn."

"Oh, Blake it sounds beautiful!"

"It is." *Was.*

Ten minutes later, Jen was covered from head to toe

with feathers. Her search as futile as mine.

"Blake, Scout could have hidden it anywhere. I have an idea. Let's systematically check the entire apartment."

Our two-bedroom, two-bathroom condo was almost two thousand square feet. That was a lot of territory to scour. With feathers scattered everywhere, it was like looking for a needle in a haystack, but Jen's plan made sense. I'd get down on my hands and knees, looking under all the furniture and rugs while she'd run the vacuum, hoping to suck it up.

One painstaking hour and ten feather-filled vacuum bags later, still nothing. Zippo. We'd scoured every square inch of the apartment and I'd even emptied out the stinky trash and dug through it piece by piece with my bare hands.

"Blake, it's got to be here," insisted my wife, optimism in her voice.

"Where!?" I barked, then apologized for sounding so gruff. I was so pissed off I could punch a wall. Or strangle *that* dog.

My compassionate tiger forgave my wrath and gave me an encouraging kiss on my cheek. "Why don't we ask him?"

Was she serious? Before I could utter a word, all sixty pounds of him came bounding into the kitchen, creating a maelstrom of feathers. He made a beeline for the emptied trash.

"Sit, Scout," Jen commanded.

Amazingly, he did as she asked and then Jen squatted down in front of him and pet his head affectionately.

"Good boy. Now, show Mommy where you hid Daddy's present."

The beast cocked his head. He stared at her with wonderment, his big brown eyes as round as marbles. He belched. Then, farted. The stinkiest, most repulsive fart I'd ever encountered. I'm talking gas mask worthy. A ten on the Richter Scale of Farts. Silent but deadly.

"Oh my God! What's that smell?" gasped Jen. Contorting her face, she looked at me and the second her gaze met mine, it hit me. Hard like a brick to my head.

"Holy shit! He ate it!" My hand flew to my forehead with a thunderous palm slap. I didn't know if I wanted to scream, cry, or bang my head against a wall. Or kill the goddamn dog!

Before I had the chance to do the latter, Scout scampered off, his tail between his legs. Panic set in.

"Blake, are you sure?" asked Jen.

"Positive!"

"What are we going to do?"

I paced the room. Scout's flatulence lingered. "I don't know."

Darkness fell over my tiger like a storm cloud. She curled her fingers against her mouth as if she was going to bite off her nails. "Blake, he's going to die! We need to get him to a vet!"

My wife seemed way more upset about the loss of the stupid dog than the loss of the beautiful bauble. Her eyes began to water.

"Call your mother! Please! She must know someone!"

Sixty seconds later, my mother was on my cell.

"Well, hello darling! How nice of you to call your dear old mother!"

I had no time for niceties.

She continued. "Mother told me she saw you last night."

And I had no time—or desire—to get into the regrettable Grandma incident. What happened yesterday seemed like a century ago.

"Mom, I have a medical emergency."

"Blake, darling! You should be calling 911, not me!"

"It's not me. It's our dog."

The alarm in her voice morphed into curiosity. "Oh, you and Jennifer got a dog? How wonderful! What's its name?"

"Scout." It was time to cut to the chase. "Mom, I need the name and phone number of the vet you used to go to."

"You mean, Dr. Rowland?

How the hell should I know? "Yeah."

"Do you know he was the vet to the stars?"

I raked my free hand through my hair. *Who gives a shit?* "Mom, I just need his number."

"I could give it to you, darling, but it's worthless."

"What do you mean?"

"He's retired! Marty lives in Palm Springs now."

Standing next to me, her face taut as a stretched rubber band, Jen mouthed for me to ask her to recommend someone else. I did as she asked.

"Darling, even if I could, no regular veterinarian would be open at this hour on a Saturday, no less. You need to take your new dog to an emergency animal hospital."

I inwardly blew out a breath of frustration. Why was extracting information from my mother always so difficult?

"Can you tell me one to go to?"

"Your father and I adore the West Los Angeles VCA. We took Mitzi there one time after she ate the entire box of Valentine's Day chocolates he bought me. They treated her like a princess! Complete with a paper crown. And then another time, we took Monique in after she stepped on a shard of glass. The poor darling! Yelping like—"

I cut her off. My mother could go on for hours with stories about her beloved, pampered poodles. I think she spent more time talking about them than about my sister and me combined.

Five minutes later, still dressed in what we'd worn

out to dinner, my anxious tiger and I were back in my car. Scout in the front seat, squeezed in beside her. On our way to the animal hospital.

"Blake, can't you go any faster?"

"Baby, I'm going as fast as I can." Though the hospital was just a few miles away, the Saturday night traffic on Wilshire Boulevard—in fact anywhere in LA—was impossible. With cops waiting to issue DUIs littered everywhere.

"Please hurry!" Tears in her voice, she wrapped her arm around the beast. "Hang in there, baby boy!"

What about me? My cock, Mr. Burns, was as deflated as our once fluffy pillows.

Getting laid tonight was no longer part of the plan.

Then, another silent but deadly fart saturated the air.

Chapter 12
Blake

The VCA Animal Hospital was a large, nondescript three-story building on Sepulveda, just south of Santa Monica Boulevard. We parked the car in the underground garage and took the elevator up to the third floor reception area, me holding a rambunctious, sniffing-everything Scout tightly by his leash. I was surprised by how many people and their pets—dogs, cats, rabbits, and more—were sitting anxiously on the scattered seating. I even heard a bird chirping. Pulling me, Scout led us to the check-in desk.

A big-boned redheaded woman sat behind the console facing her massive computer. She reminded me a lot of the obnoxious woman who'd admitted me to Cedars when I'd had my scary bout of priapism a few months back. Maybe they were sisters or separated at birth. Same frizzy red hair. Except this one wore glasses.

"Please sign in with your name and your pet's as well as your time of arrival." She barely looked at me and as I did as I was told, she asked, "What is your dog's problem?"

Jen responded, her voice frantic. "He ate a piece of jewelry and may die!"

The woman looked up at us, then over the frames of her half-moon glasses, gazed down at our unfazed Scout. Her thin lips twisted in sync with an eyeroll. "It happens often."

Jen paled, her face awash with terror. Even my stomach twitched. What did Frizzbitch mean by that? That jewelry consumption among canines was common and lead to consequential death?

My thoughts were cut short by another silent but deadly Scout fart. Whoa! The odor that wafted in the air was so foul that the person standing behind me moved ten feet away. If farts could kill, this would be it.

Scrunching her nose, Frizzbitch shot me a disgusted look. "Please take a seat and we'll call you when it's your turn. Except for dire emergencies, it's first come, first serve."

Well, at least we had a little reassurance that Scout wasn't on his deathbed. My eyes circled the waiting room. There were at least a dozen people ahead of us. The wait would be long. We could be here all night. And into the morning.

We took a seat, and Scout lay down in front of us. He seemed unusually lethargic. Jen squeezed my free hand, hers cold and clammy. Her other hand brushed across Scout's coat.

"It's going to be okay, baby boy." She caressed him again. "Mommy's here."

Despite her continuous strokes, the dog didn't move. Not even the twitch of an ear. His muzzle rested on his outstretched front legs, his tail curled behind him. I'd be lying if I said he looked happy. His big brown eyes seemed a bit glazed. Maybe he was just bored. My tiger, however, filled with alarm.

"Blake, he's fading!" Tears sprung to her eyes, then she burst into sobs.

Several people in the reception area turned around to look at her. She was a blubbering mess. Nothing I could say or do could console her. Reaching into my back pocket, I handed her one of my monogrammed hankies. She blew her nose, dabbed her tears, and then sniffled a few words.

"Blake, please call your mother again. Maybe she knows someone here."

The last thing I wanted to do was call my mother again. But my tiger's sobs were gutting me, so I did as she asked. It turned out my parents had made a substantial donation to the animal hospital several years ago and my mother was still very friendly with the Chief of Staff. Yup, money had its benefits. And so did connections.

We were the next to be called.

The examination room was small and sterile. Just an exam table, a few cabinets, a sink with nearby disinfectants, a counter filled with sundry medical supplies. And one solitary chair, which I insisted Jen take, while I stood holding Scout by his leash. He seemed to have rebounded. Once again inquisitive and happy. Wagging his tail and longing to explore everything.

My tiger had stopped crying, but her eyes were puffy and red-rimmed. She was still fraught with worry. Nervously, she fiddled with her diamond snowflake engagement ring, her hands wringing in her lap. "Blake, do you think Scout's going to be okay?"

Though he seemed fine, who knew? I was not a medical doctor. My instinct was to say yes to make my wife feel better and so I selfishly didn't have to deal with more gut-wrenching bawling. Before I could respond, the door to the room swung open, and a raspy voice sounded.

"Hey, there. I'm Dr. Sexton, but most call me by my first name Chase. Dr. Chase."

Both Jen and I looked up. Heading our way was an extremely good-looking guy, tall and athletically built and about my age. Under his white lab coat, he was wearing well-cut jeans and a Snoopy T-shirt that hinted of his pronounced pecs and washboard abs. A stethoscope was wrapped around his neck and a pair of expensive Nikes adorned his feet. With his build, perfectly tousled light brown hair, bedroom-blue eyes, chiseled face with its designer scruff, I swear he looked like he'd just stepped out of *GQ*, lab attire and all. Or could be the star of a TV series. Somehow, he looked familiar to me. And his name was too. Where did I know him from? Before I could search my mind, he offered me his hand, and I shook it with my free one, introducing myself and Jen. His grip was firm and confident, his fingers long and tapered. Then, he shook Jen's, and a blast of jealousy whipped through me when she gave him a warm smile.

"Dr. Chase, thank you for seeing us!"

He returned her smile. It was one of those dazzling Hollywood ones. Slightly lopsided with a row of sparkling white straight teeth. I was ready to blow this pop stand. Or punch out those pearly whites.

Letting go of Jen's hand, he squatted and stroked Scout with his large hands.

"So you must be Scout." The dog held his gaze and wagged his tail. "I heard you got into some mischief tonight."

Jen explained how Scout had torn through our apartment. She still had a few feathers stuck to the fabric of her dress, which she picked off like lint. "And then, Doctor, he chewed up a little box and ate a broach!" Terror inched back into Jen's voice. "My birthday present."

Still squatting, the vet checked the beast's heartbeat with his stethoscope and then stood to fetch a thermometer. He squatted again, this time behind Scout.

"You're not going to like this, buddy, but trust me, it'll only last a few seconds." I cringed as he lifted Scout's butt up a little and inserted the thermometer into his poop hole. Poor Scout whimpered, alarming Jen further.

"Doctor, is he going to die?"

Wordlessly, he removed the thermometer and studied it. Then, he chuckled. "No, he's way too young and healthy. There's nothing to worry about."

"Seriously?" I said, my brows lifting.

"Seriously." His voice was confident and reassuring. "You know what they say: what goes in, must come out. I am going to give him an all-natural laxative which will help him poop out the broach, hopefully later tonight." He headed toward the door. "Hang tight. I'll be right back."

Letting go of the leash, I let Scout prowl about the small room. He seemed back to his sniffing, rambunctious, tail-wagging self. And for the first time since the start of this ordeal, Jen seemed back to herself. Relaxed and happy.

"Blake, I *really* like Dr. Chase!"

I made a face. "You do?"

She smiled. "Yes. He seems super-smart and exudes

confidence."

And sex appeal? I silently added, knitting my brows.

"And he's really cute."

I felt my blood bubbling. I did not like where this conversation was going. Not one bit.

"I wonder if he's married."

"What does it matter?" I snapped, not having noticed if he was wearing a wedding band. Or not.

"Well, I was just thinking . . ."

Before she could finish her sentence, Dr. Pretty Face came jogging back into the room. Happy to see him, Scout wagged his tail and my tiger gave him the kind of smile she wore after we had epic, toe-curling sex. I felt my blood pressure spike. What the hell was she thinking?

"Sorry to keep you guys, waiting," my new nemesis said, dipping his hand into one of his lab coat pockets. He slipped it out and in his palm were two tablets that resembled dog treats.

"What are those?" asked Jen.

"A laxative. Poopies."

"P-O-O-P-I-E-S?"

Chase laughed. A goddamn sexy laugh! "No, Poop-Ease. E-A-S-E."

"Oh!" Jen blushed.

"They'll soften Scout's stool and make it easier for him to poop out the broach. They contain all natural ingredients, including sugar beet and flaxseed. Dogs love them!" He turned to Scout, who had his face buried in the corner. "Come here, Scout." Chase bent down and held his hand out. "Look what I have for you!"

In a flash, Scout was sitting before the vet, voraciously eating the tablets out of his hand. As if they were candy.

With the hand that fed him, Chase pat the dog's head. "Good boy!" He then stood up and faced me.

"That should do the trick! You'll likely have your broach within the next twenty-four hours."

"What if he doesn't poop it out?" My voice was dripping with distrust.

"I'm going to give you a jar of Poop-Ease to take home. Give Scout two chews every three hours until he does. Just be sure to keep the jar away from him. If he ingests too many of them, you'll have a *real* life-threatening emergency on your hands."

Death by Diarrhea, I silently snickered. This pain-in-the-ass dog could have a nice abbreviated life. And be out of mine. Jen cut my evil thoughts short.

"Isn't it going to hurt him?" she asked, worry back in her voice. "I mean the pooping part. The broach is a platinum unicorn with a diamond cone."

"Hmm, sounds like your husband has good taste."

I smiled smugly, but that didn't make me like him any better as he elaborated.

"Worst case scenario, the cone may tear his rectum a little and he'll shed a little blood. Swallowing chicken and steak bones, which happens all the time, can have the same effect. I'll also give you an antibiotic in case that happens, and I'll want you to bring him back or go to your local vet for a check up."

"We don't have a vet yet," I said.

"Dr. Chase, can *you* be our vet?" The plea in my tiger's voice sounded something between smitten and wishful like all those pimply middle school girls who asked me to be their boyfriend on Valentine's Day. Jealousy again reared its ugly green-eyed head.

A huge megawatt smile beamed on his pretty face. *Kill me now!* Reword: *Kill him now!* "I'd be honored to and the timing couldn't be more perfect. I'm opening my own practice next week in Culver City and you'll be among my first patients."

Culver City? That's where Conquest Broadcasting was located. That meant his new office was likely not far from ours. Probably just a few minutes away by car . . . which meant that my tiger could easily step out of the office for a little doggie-style tryst in one of his examining rooms or his private office. I felt my blood boil. The sooner we got out of here the better. Because I might wring this guy's neck or do some other bodily harm. My mind raced as my blood pressure rose. I might have to eliminate him! Just the way I'd eliminated Jen's douchebag dentist fiancé, Bradley Wick, with

Operation Dickwick. Now, I had to put a new plan into effect. What should I call it? Operation Chaseman? Chaseaway? Chaseface? I stared at his smug chiseled face and—boom!—it came to me like a hailstorm in the summer. Operation Chasehole! Perfection! But it wasn't going to be easy because this asswipe wasn't the clueless moron Dickwick was. He had charm. He had looks. And from the looks of it, he had balls.

As I clenched my fists and simmered, pretty-face Chase told us we could pick up Scout's prescriptions at the front desk. Jen thanked him cheerfully. I was eager to get home. And to get this fricking dog to take a dump. My obsession with Chasehole had almost made me forget the reason we'd come here.

Just as I was about to say adieu, Chasehole stopped me in my tracks.

"Hey, Blake. Did you by chance go to UCLA? Class of '95?"

"Yeah, why?"

"I graduated from UCLA that year too. You were on the track team with me ... but I don't remember your last name being Burns."

Ah-ha! That's how I knew him! I told him my last name used to be the same as my father's—Bernstein—but that I'd changed it for professional reasons. I didn't get into my male modeling stint—something that was long in the past, yet every once in a while came back to bite me in the ass when some crazed woman recognized me and practically tore my clothes off.

"You looked familiar too." I remembered him now. As good looking and as athletic as he was, he kept to himself, studying in the library and not partying with the rest of us. "Your last name is familiar too. What does your father do?"

"He's an accountant . . . Charles Sexton."

"You mean like the Sexton in Sexton and Meyers?" That was my father's accounting firm and Charles Sexton was his personal accountant. They had offices all over the country. While not quite the billionaire my old man was, his father was loaded.

"Yes," replied Chasehole, who was becoming less of a real threat to me. Thank fuck, he didn't go by the name Dr. Sex.

"My real name is actually Charles—Charles Sexton the Third—but I've been Chase for as long as I remember. I didn't want to follow in my father's footsteps."

Neither did I, but here I was being groomed to be the next head of Conquest Broadcasting. I had to say I've never for one day regretted working for my old man. Though we had totally different ways of doing business—I shot from my gut; he was methodical—I admired and learned a lot from him. He was a brilliant businessman and respected leader, and I looked forward to our weekly chats on his terrace, drinking bourbon and smoking cigars, talking about life and the biz. And

I had much to thank him for. If he hadn't hired my tiger, I would have likely never seen her again after that unforgettable blindfolded kiss.

Chasehole continued, breaking into my mental ramblings. "I never wanted to be a bean counter. I've always loved animals and for as long as I can remember, I've wanted to be a vet. After I graduated UCLA, I attended UC-Davis, which has one of the best veterinary medicine programs in the country."

"That's wonderful," beamed Jen. "And it's so exciting you're opening your own practice."

"Yeah, I'm excited about it too. I'm going to miss this place, but it's time. And my dream. I'm putting an emphasis on holistic medicine and natural, organic products. On the way out, I'll also give you a sample of the organic dog food I recommend. Dogs love it—and it really helps them regulate their bowel movements. You can buy it on Chewy.com and I'll also be stocking it at my new office."

"I will and I love Chewy!" gushed Jen. "Oh, and by the way, if you need an assistant or receptionist, I know the perfect one."

Scrunching my brows. I wondered whom she was talking about. No one in our family or circle of friends stood out.

"I might," replied Chase. "Can you get us in touch?"

Jen's face brightened. "I will!"

"Great! Here's my new business card." He reached into a pocket and handed one to Jen. "And one last thing, given the damage Scout caused in your house tonight with his rowdy behavior, I highly recommend you get him into training right away."

"What do you mean?" I asked.

"Enroll him in obedience school. There's a great class that meets in Roxbury Park every Sunday morning. A new session is starting tomorrow." He wrote down a name and web address on a scrap of paper and handed it to me. "Tell Martha I sent you and she'll give you a discount."

"Thanks." Internally, I growled. I hated school and the last thing I wanted to do on a Sunday morning was go to school with the beast. At least, Jen would be there, too, and when the instructor wasn't looking, I could squeeze her ass or pinch her tits.

"And one final last thing, take Scout for a walk as soon as you get home. If the laxative doesn't work, try again tomorrow morning. Good luck and keep me posted."

"Isn't he the best?" gushed Jen as we took the elevator down to the parking structure. "I'm crazy about him!"

She was back to gushing over the damn dog who'd already cost me close to two thousand smackereroos. Make that twenty-five if I didn't get the broach back.

"Do you mean Scout?" I asked snarkily.

"No, I mean Dr. Chase."

I felt my muscles clenching. I was just beginning to like the guy, and now jealousy was pouring back into my veins like hot lava.

"And did you notice he wasn't wearing a wedding band?"

"I wasn't paying attention." All my attention had been on the two of them, exchanging flirtatious smiles.

"I bet he's single! He's so cute!"

Seriously!? Mental palm slap. *Give me a frigging break!*

"He'd be perfect for Libby!"

"Yeah, he'd be perfect for her!" I readily agreed. And they should move to Zimbabwe, take care of endangered animals, and live happily ever after. Libby could even conduct focus groups with monkeys. Under the influence, she could talk to anyone and anything about everything.

As the elevator reached our parking level and the doors slid open, I made a new mental note: Find another vet or find a way to get rid of this dog.

Or both.

Chapter 13
Blake

It was close to midnight when we got home. Jen and I quickly changed into sweats and our running shoes while a thirsty Scout slurped up some water in the kitchen. Five minutes later, we were out the door with Scout on his leash. Jen was carrying a tote filled with plastic bags, bottles of water, and a pair of chopsticks. Scout was filled with boundless energy, eager to take a walk. Over an hour had passed since he'd taken the laxative and fingers crossed its magic would work.

Heading east on still busy, high rise-lined Wilshire, we made a right turn onto a side street, which led us into a neighborhood of well-groomed older, moderate-sized houses with front lawns and tree-lined sidewalks.

'This is a pretty neighborhood," commented Jen.

"Yeah, it is." Surprisingly, for as long as I'd lived on the Wilshire Corridor, I'd never explored the surrounding area.

"Would you want to live here?"

"What do you mean?"

"I mean like buy a house here."

"I don't think so." While the houses had curb appeal, they were too on top of each other for my taste. And too small. While I didn't want to live in a palatial mansion or a gated community like my parents, I wanted something that was more spacious and with more property... and preferably close to the Santa Monica steps and the beach. There was a street called Adelaide that I loved, but in all the years I'd parked along it, I'd rarely seen a *For Sale* sign.

"I'd love to buy something on Adelaide," I told Jen. She loved that street, too, as the houses reminded her of the grand houses in Des Moines. Though what sold for five hundred thousand dollars there was probably five million here. Real estate prices in Los Angeles, especially close to the ocean, were astronomical. Even a small two-bedroom cottage close to the beach sold for a million dollars or more.

"Could we afford to?" My wife still hadn't gotten used to my wealth and still shopped at moderately priced stores, seeking out sales and bargains. Something she had in common with my grandma and bonded them.

"We can afford just about anything."

A long stretch of silence followed. We continued to walk, with Scout stopping to sniff whatever he fancied. So far, he'd lifted his leg twice to pee, but nothing had inspired him to take a dump. It was getting chilly and I was getting fed up. We'd been outside for over a half hour.

"I don't think that laxative stuff is working," I grumbled. All hope of getting back the broach was evaporating like water. And my faith in this quack doctor was waning exponentially.

"You have to be patient, Blake." My tiger hugged herself to stay warm. "Dr. Chase said it could take several tries."

Patience was not one of my virtues. I was ready to turn back when Scout began circling a patch of grass.

Jen glommed on to my arm. "Blake, I think he's going to make a poop!"

My eyes stayed fixed on him as he squatted. *C'mon, boy, sock it to me!* He squeezed out whatever was inside him, then stood up, vigorously kicking his hind legs behind him, covering the turd with a tuft of dirt and grass.

"Blake, do you see the broach?" my wife asked excitedly.

On the dark, dimly lit street, it was hard to see shit (no pun intended), especially now that *it* was camouflaged by nature. I carefully circled it, hoping not to step in it. I knew I was close because the stench drifted up my nose. Ugh! It rivaled his flatulence. I squatted down. Nothing that sparkled met my eyes.

"Jen, can you hold his leash while I look?"

"Sure." She took it from me as I pulled out my cell

phone and turned on the flashlight, aiming it at the giant turd. "Give me one of the chopsticks."

Holding my breath and on to the tiniest glimmer of hope, I poked an end of the wooden stick into the giant pile of shit, then began swirling it around, trying to uncover the missing bauble. Hoping to see the tip of the unicorn's diamond cone peek through. The stench was overwhelming. "UGH!" I choked, wishing I'd brought along one of the scarves we'd brought in Scotland to wrap around my face and ward off the vomiticious smell. Vomiticious was a word made up by Jennifer, but it had become part of my vocabulary.

I swirled and I swirled and I swirled with what I was now dubbing the Shitstick. Some clever telemarketer could probably package them and turn them into an *As Seen on TV* product. And make a bloody fortune. I could hear his voice in my head . . . "And that's not all. They're washable. Reusable. Recyclable. Use them for anything . . . from dog shit to sushi."

God, I was genius, but then Jen cut into my mental ramblings. And into my swelling ego. "Do you see anything?"

Squinting, I shook my head. I swirled some more. Nothing. I was losing hope. Nada. Absolutely fucking nada. For all I knew, the broach had dissolved in the beast's stomach, destroyed by his lethal gastric acids. Rising to my feet, I let out a loud, exasperated breath. It sounded like a deflating balloon. "Let's go home, baby.

Tomorrow's another day."

After tossing the Shitstick into the nearest trash bin along with a bagful of dog shit, we walked back to our condo, me holding Scout's leash in one hand, Jen's hand in the other. Our fingers were threaded.

"Tiger, maybe he'll poop out the broach tomorrow after we give him another dose of the laxative." I knew I didn't sound convincing as I didn't believe my own words.

Jen squeezed my hand. "Blake, it's not that important. I know the broach means a lot to you, but that's not what matters to me. Scout's alive. You're alive. We have each other—that's all we need. I love you so much and I know you love me."

Her heartfelt words resonated deep inside me. I stopped in my tracks, holding a boisterous Scout back with all I had.

"Look at me, baby." She turned to face me, and on my next breath, I curled my free arm around her waist, drawing her close to me. The full moon shining upon us.

"Happy Birthday, tiger." Maybe it was already the next day, but who gave a shit, no pun intended. "I *do* love you. So fucking much." Then, I tilted up her chin so I could swoop down and give her a hot, passionate kiss. The gnawing, sucking, lip-bruising you-are-mine kind. She moaned against my mouth just as Scout tugged at the leash. I had no choice but to let go of her and head back to our condo. Despite how much I hated this dog, I felt better. My tiger's lips had healing powers. Like a balm.

Scout was happy to be home. Bypassing the night doorman, he burst inside our building, sliding across the marble floor to the elevators as if he was speed skating on ice. Jen and I were running an Olympic six-meter race to keep up with him. The elevator doors pinged open and we followed a panting Scout inside it.

Breathless, we reached our apartment and I undid the deadbolt with my key.

"Baby boy, we're home," breathed Jen, glancing down at Scout the Jewel Thief.

I pushed the door open, but the beast just stood there. Like he was suddenly unsure if he wanted to go inside. And then he squatted.

"Oh no!" shrieked Jen, her face aghast.

That familiar awful stench drifted up my nose and then I looked down.

Christ. He'd made a deposit, this one gross and liquidy. Diarrhea. But lo and behold, diamonds glittered in my eyes.

Holy shit! No pun intended! He'd at last pooped out the broach!

"Way to go!" I commended, patting him as I bent down to retrieve it from the steaming puddle of poo. I didn't give a flying fuck that shit was all over my fingers. The broach was in my possession!

"Oh my God! The broach!" Jen was as excited as I was and kept up with me as I hurried to the kitchen sink to wash it off. Along with my fingers. First with some dishwashing soap and warm water, then with a non-abrasive scouring pad. Using a soft clean dishcloth, I dried it off. Wow! The unicorn broach was more beautiful than I remembered. With its platinum body, emerald eyes (the color of Jen's), and sparkling pave diamond cone.

All cleaned up, I held it in the palm of my hand as Jen gazed down at it. Her jaw dropped and her eyes widened with awe.

"Oh, Blake, it's so beautiful!"

I reflected on its significance as I pinned it onto her hoodie.

On our tour of Edinburgh, we'd passed a famous bronze statue of a unicorn, and our personal guide had explained that while the animal is mythological, the ideals it represents made it the perfect choice, fit to be the national animal of Scotland. And because like this proud beast, Scots would fight to remain unconquered. While I was finger-fucking Jen beneath her tiny kilt, half listening, something had sunk in. I identified with unicorns. Their fearlessness was much like the *That Man* I was. Plus, they were a symbol of good luck. Unicorns made dreams come true. Perhaps one would bring us a baby. So, when I saw this antique jeweled one in the window of a small shop in the city's charming West End district, I knew I had to have it despite the exorbitant price. The kind, elderly proprietor told me that the previous owner had given it to his infertile wife and she subsequently produced three heirs. That sealed the deal. When I left the shop, the box was in my pocket.

Without getting into details, I told Jen what unicorns symbolized. She kept her eyes on the broach. "It *will* bring us good luck, Blake. It already has."

"It has?"

"It's brought us the best fur baby in the world." She paused reflectively. "And I know, just know, our dream of having a child will come true."

Scout, who had followed us into the kitchen, barked twice.

Perhaps, he was seconding her wish.

Jen looped her arms around my neck.

"Thank you, my love, for the best birthday ever."

There was a mess to clean up by the front door, but I was going to let it go.

And make my tiger's birthday even better.

Chapter 14
Blake

The Royal Canine Obedience School was held in Roxbury Park on Pico close to Conquest Broadcasting and a mere fifteen minute drive from my condo, given there was little traffic on a Sunday morning. I'd wanted Jen to come along, but she was meeting with her new speech coach. A rising star at Conquest Broadcasting with many important presentations and interviews ahead of her, it was suggested by both my father and our head of Public Relations that she consult with one and embellish her public speaking skills. Wanting to go far in the company, she agreed to their suggestion.

I found parking easily and marched Scout through the grass. Or should I say he marched me, tugging at his leash. The ground muddy, we left footmarks in our tracks.

"Hey, bud, sorry you have to go to school on a Sunday," I muttered out loud, thinking about all the weekend detentions I'd had to endure as a kid, all the way through high school. Scout didn't seem to mind one bit. Sniffing everything, he chugged ahead, stopping only to lift his leg a few times until we reached our destination.

I followed the signs. The school was located in a shady area just outside the adult community center. In the near distance, there was a children's park filled with swings, a sandbox, seesaws, and benches. It was already crowded with kids and their parents. Close to the community center, older men and women, dressed in all white, were playing a leisurely game of bocce ball. Lawn bowling as it was called here.

I recognized the instructor from the school's website. Her name was Martha Churchill. She was a stout, middle-aged woman, with cropped gray coarse hair, a square jaw, and handsome features, and outfitted in khaki Bermuda shorts, hiking boots, and a sweatshirt with a silhouette of a crown-bearing dog—the school's logo. A wide-brimmed hat that resembled a drill sergeant's hung from her bullish neck along with a whistle suspended from a lanyard. She looked like the no nonsense, militaristic type and reminded me of my pickle-up-her-butt homeroom teacher, Mrs. Aston (aka Mrs. Asshat), who followed me through high school and threatened to have me expelled for being perennially late and throwing spitballs. Lucky for me, too bad for her, my parents were major donors of the posh private school I attended. Every morning she was reminded when we did our daily convocation in the Saul and Helen Bernstein Auditorium.

"Welcome. I'm your instructor, Miss Churchill." Her pitchy voice was clearly British and I'd have to say rather snooty. She gave Scout and me the once-over. "Please introduce yourselves."

Her tone curt, I did as she asked.

"Very well. Please take your places by one of the remaining yellow triangles. Our class is going to be delightfully small. Only five students. We're expecting just one other."

All but one of her clients, including me, was already there. A shaggy-haired surfer type with his equally scruffy mutt . . . a twenty-something Valley-girl type who childishly wore her sandy-blond hair in pigtails and looked a lot like her floppy-eared cocker spaniel . . . a middle-aged, pug-faced woman who bore a close resemblance to her snorting pug. And lastly, a buzzed-cut, tattooed forty-ish dude wearing a U.S. Marines wife-beater and holding his ferocious looking pit bull tight on a thick metal link chain that looped around his powerful neck. It looked like it belonged on a high-security barbed wire fence. The dog was also wearing a black leather collar with gunmetal spikes that resembled bullets.

Holding Scout tightly by his leash, I hesitantly took my place next to the duo.

"Hey, dude! Welcome to the class. I'm Boyd."

"Cool. I'm Blake."

"Nice lookin' dog you have. What's his name?"

I introduced Scout as I studied his dog. Built just like his owner. Big and brawny, the size of his balls rivaling that of his jaw. "What's your dog's name?"

"Attila."

"Like in Attila the Hun?" From my vague recollection of ancient history, he was a ruthless barbarian who stopped at nothing.

With a proud shit-eating grin, Boyd reached down to give his barbarian beast a firm pat. "Yup, that's my boy! A pure bred American Staffordshire Terrier."

Terrier my ass. This dog was a deadly assault weapon. Ready to launch.

On cue, the beast returned the shit-eating grin, bearing his monstrous fangs. A shiver ran through me as Boyd ordered his "boy" to sit.

On command, Attila did as his master asked. Better than sic me, right?

"He seems very obedient," I observed nervously. "Why are you taking this class?"

"Oh, it's just a refresher course. Attila's done it a dozen times. It keeps him in check. He had a small setback this week and bit the mailman. The dude had to get six stitches. No biggie, but better safe than sorry, right?"

"Right." I glanced down at my feet. I was wearing Nikes and sweats. A plan of self-defense formulated in my head. If this ankle-biting beast dare try to attack me, I'd kick him hard in the face, and then get the hell out of here as fast as my legs would let me. With Scout or without him, though it would make sense to have him close by for protection.

A loud harrumph cut into my thoughts. My gaze jumped to our instructor, who was standing with her legs straddled and arms folded. She was glancing down at her watch. Yup, she was for sure a by-the-book type. Anal as anal could be. I'd bet big money she was a drill sergeant in her former life. Whip and all.

She scrunched her face. "It's five minutes past the hour. Let's not wait for our other student and begin." Her steely eyes zoomed in on Scout and me. "Mr. Burns, please put Scout's choke chain on him."

Huh? What was she talking about? Scout had on his nice red leather collar that matched his leash.

My new pal Boyd elbowed me, pointing to Attila's intimidating metal link collar. "This kind of thing."

I met Churchill's fierce gaze. "Um, we don't have one."

Scowling, she narrowed her eyes at me and planted her hands on her matronly hips. "Mr. Burns, didn't you read the prerequisites for the course? It clearly states that all dogs and owners are required to come with a choke chain."

I gulped while oblivious Scout wagged his tail. "I must have missed that." Fearing a lash of her whip, which I was sure she was hiding in a pocket, I dared not tell her I never went beyond the website's home page.

Martha eased her stance, relaxing her dour expression just a bit. "Very well. You're here, but just know that without a choke chain, this lesson is basically a waste of your time. And mine." She paused, checking her watch once again. "Let's begin."

For the next twenty minutes, we ran through a series of commands: sit, down, and stay. Despite not wearing a choke chain, Scout did well with sit and down. But for the life of him, he couldn't master stay. Every time I walked twenty feet away from him and shouted stay which was accompanied by a stop-sign like hand gesture, he sat there for a moment, his head cocked in confusion, then sprung into action, charging toward me, never giving me the chance to say one of my favorite words: "Come!" To my dismay and embarrassment, the other pet owners and their dogs had no problem mastering this command.

Drill sergeant Martha looked at me disapprovingly. *Kill me now.* "Mr. Burns, I'd like you to try the stay and come commands one more time before we move on."

Reluctantly, recovering my mojo and feeling all eyes on me, I did as she asked, distancing myself from Scout once again. I looked him straight in the eye, hoping he could read my mind. *C'mon, boy. Show your stuff. Don't be a dog school flunky.*

"Stay," I said affirmatively, holding my hand up.

He did as I asked. I kept my hand up for a good thirty seconds, and to my amazement, he didn't budge. *Good boy!* Pride rose inside me and then, as I parted my lips about to say "come," a familiar indignant voice trilled in my ears.

"Ugh! How dare you call yourself the Royal Canine Obedience School? This place is for peasants!"

All eyes turned toward the shrill voice. Showing his teeth, Attila growled.

"Excuse me," huffed Martha as my gaze veered too. "Who the hell are you? And how dare you interrupt my class in progress?"

Stumbling our way, as her six-inch heels sunk into the damp, spongy grass, was a tall, lanky, stylishly dressed woman, wearing a big floppy straw hat over her shoulder-length platinum hair. Despite her face being obscured, I'd recognize her anywhere.

Shitballs!

It was the psycho bitch! The last person I ever wanted to see again!

Katrina Moore! My bat crazy ex-girlfriend who had stalked me, drugged me, and tried to stop me from marrying my tiger. I hadn't seen her since my wedding, the first and disastrous one, which landed Jen in the hospital with a life-threatening ovarian cyst. As my father always said: *Out of sight, out of mind.* What the hell was she doing here?

Though she didn't notice me, my eyes stayed riveted on her as she staggered toward us, grunting and cursing with every unsteady step. A monstrous pink designer bag dangled from one arm, and as she got closer, I noticed something peeking out from inside it . . . a small white furry dog. It sported a frou frou pink bow on its head and a matching pink rhinestone collar.

Martha's gruff voice jolted me. "Mr. Burns, please stop focusing on this riff-raff. Your dog is still sitting patiently and waiting for you to call him."

Impulsively, turning my attention away from Katrina, I called out to Scout.

"Scout, *come!*"

Scout's eyes lit up. Not wasting a second, he bolted my way, except he didn't stop. He blew past me, not slowing his pace. I spun around and my eyes grew wide. Holy Moses! He was making a beeline for Katrina! And her little white dog!

"Scout, *stop!*" I hollered at the top of my lungs, trying to make myself heard above Attila's now fierce, relentless yelps.

Stop was obviously not in my dog's repertoire of commands. I didn't blink once as Katrina's dog jumped out of her bag. With a yap, he scampered away as her eyeballs ping-ponged between my incoming dog and her outgoing one.

"Gucci!" she cried out. "You bad dog! Get your furry butt back here! Right now!"

It was futile. The little dog kept running as if its ass

was on fire and the nearest water was a mile away. Yipping gleefully. As it had never left the confines of Katrina's purse before and experienced freedom.

"Get back here!" she repeated before frantically turning to Martha and then to the class. "Do something! Anyone!"

No one budged. Though Scout kept going. But rather than chasing after the white bouncing ball of fur, he pounced upon Katrina, knocking her to the ground. Flat on her back, spread out like a starfish, she let out another ear-piercing shriek. Pinning her down with his weight, Scout began to gnaw her pebbled leather bag.

"Oh my God! Get this savage beast off me! He's destroying my twenty-five thousand dollar Birkin!!"

Rawhide! I silently chortled, almost laughing out loud. Haha! One slut's treasure is some other's mutt's treat! *Go for it, boy!* I silently cheered him on.

"Let go, you ugly beast!" Katrina screamed, now playing tug of war with the bag, which only made Scout more determined, more playful, more aggressive. He was having fun!

"Someone, call this beast off!" she implored, having no regard for her little fuzzy dog who was now frolicking in the grass like it'd never had fun or playtime.

Call me a sadist, but I was enjoying every second of this spectacle. Finally, after a few minutes, I strode over to her. Her frantic eyes shot up at me, glinting with recognition.

"Blake, what the hell are you doing here?"

"Same thing you are. Enjoying the 'fall' weather." Adjusting my baseball cap, I paused for a beat. "Have you met my new dog, Scout?"

She looked down, her eyes crossed, and then her expression grew horrified. Scout was chewing off the handle of her bag. It was tethered only by a leather sliver. She shrieked again.

"Oh my God! He's totally destroyed my Birkin! Do you know how rare this bag is? How long I waited to get it!?" With every word, her voice grew shriller, more enraged.

Before I could respond, another familiar voice thundered in my ears.

"OFF!" commanded Martha. She gave Scout's hind side a firm but gentle whack and he bounded off. I managed to grab his leash before he leapt away.

"Thank God." Slowly, Katrina sat up and rose to her feet, grabbing what remained of her Hermès bag. The leather tattered; the handle dangling by a thread. Then, she glanced down at herself. Her all-white designer duds were covered with dirt, grass stains, and paw prints. Her face again went crimson, her voice ballistic.

"You! *You!*" she barked at Martha. "Not only have you ruined my Birkin, but you've also ruined my new Armani outfit!"

Martha stood steadfast, unfazed. "So sue me."

"Just wait and see." Her face growing redder with rage, Katrina stomped off, gathering her little white fur ball in her arms.

In the background, I heard cheers from Cocker Spaniel Girl, Puglady, and Boyd.

Martha stood her ground, ready to get back to work. I looked at her earnestly.

"I'm sorry Scout cost you a client. And if she tries to sue you, I'll take care of it."

"Don't worry. She won't. She's more concerned about that obnoxious bag."

I offered to pay for it if needed. A twenty-five thousand bag was a small price to pay to get Katrina back out of my life.

"Thank you, but I hope you won't have to." Martha's voice softened while my posture remained stiff.

"At ease, Mr. Burns. That sweet little dog wasn't the problem. Nor was yours. That shrew was. Dog ownership doesn't come with entitlement. No dog, like no child, is born perfect, but an owner can work hard at making him or her the best they can be."

"How do you know that?"

"Years of training them. And life experience." She paused, her expression growing reflective. "My husband and I gave birth to a son. A highly autistic one. He was a challenge, a great one, but we were patient. And we worked with him. Painstakingly. Gave him all the socialization tools he needed. Today, at the age of twenty, Noah is enrolled in an intensive program that will enable him to become a film editor."

"Wow! That's amazing. When he graduates, let me know. I work in broadcasting and can help him find a job."

For the first time, she gave me a smile. Small but nonetheless genuine. "Thank you. I really appreciate that." Our eyes stayed locked. The connection growing deeper.

"Remember, Mr. Burns, there are no bad dogs." Her eyes dug into me. "Only bad owners. Flummoxed, wavering, weak-willed masters. Or those who don't give a damn and shouldn't own a dog in the first place."

Her words stung me. I was all of the above. Feeling glum, I half-heartedly participated in the rest of the training session. Without a choke chain, it was futile getting Scout to heel. To walk beside me at my pace. Tugging at his leash, he had his own agenda. Sensing my frustration, Martha came up to me as the class dispersed, and Scout and I were about to head back to my car.

"Don't give up, Mr. Burns. Scout has a lot of potential. He's a good dog. And a very handsome one too. I hope to see the both of you back here next Sunday."

Feeling utterly defeated, I marched back to my car. The fricking dog tugging at the leash so hard my arm hurt. He was a flunky. A dog school flunky.

The dog sergeant's words resonated in my head. Screw her! I was no weak-willed ninny. I was *That Man* . . . master of my universe. I'd show this dog who was the boss. Who was the alpha.

On the way home, we made one stop. Petco. And one purchase.

Three laps around the parking lot with his new choke chain around his neck . . . And Scout knew how to heel.

Ha! I was the boss. And he was a genius.

I'd show *her*.

Scout was on his way to being the best dog in the world.

Chapter 15
Jennifer

This was my second session with Krystal Clare, the head of the company that bore her namesake—Krystal Clare Communication. The woman Conquest Broadcasting had brought on to help me improve my public speaking skills. As a rising star within the company as the Director of My Sin-TV, Blake and his CEO father Saul Bernstein along with our Publicity Department all agreed I needed to hone my skills. I was good in front of a crowd, on a panel, and in a one-on-one-interview, but I needed to be great. *Good is the enemy of better,* preached my brilliant father-in-law and I believed him. I wanted to go far. And make both him and my husband proud.

Krystal was an attractive, fit-looking woman about my height. Probably in her late thirties, maybe early forties. It was hard to tell. Her blow-dried bobbed hair was a vibrant shade of auburn and framed her taut face like a helmet, not a strand out of place. Though it was a Sunday, her makeup was impeccable, and she wore a smart pair of black slacks and a cream silk blouse along with three-inch leather heels that matched her belt. I studied her as she set up the video equipment that would allow the both of us to observe what I was doing right. And doing wrong. There was something familiar about her, but I couldn't put my finger on it.

Krystal had insisted we work from the condo I shared with Blake. According to her, it made clients more relaxed, more responsive to be in a safe, familiar environment. And it was best if no one else was around. "Distractions," she said, "are deadly." I agreed to let Krystal come to the apartment and decided that Sunday mornings when Blake went to the gym to workout would be best.

This was our second session. The first took place just before Blake and I traveled to Scotland. And before we got Scout. She had thoughtfully brought over croissants and coffee from Starbucks and seemed nice enough though rather buttoned up. Very professional, with her hot pink pantsuit and leather briefcase. I'd managed to go on to her website, and her credentials were rather impressive. There wasn't much personal info about her like her childhood or marital status, but it did mention she was born in a small town outside of Vegas and had a dual degree in public relations and drama from the University of Nevada. It also listed many high-level executives, none of which I knew, as her clients. Their endorsements were outstanding, with most saying that she'd brought their public speaking skills' to the next level and helped them become confident, dynamic speakers whether it be before a crowd of hundreds or in an intimate interview with a business watchdog. All attested to her clever play-on-words motto: *Make it Krystal Clare. Confidence begins with you!*

Over the Starbucks goodies, Krystal had laid out what she wanted to accomplish with me. She was straightforward, blunt, and to the point. She'd viewed my upfront presentation from last April, a keynote speech given at the annual Women in Hollywood's luncheon, as well as a YouTube interview with one of *Variety's* top reporters. While she thought I sounded articulate and intelligent, my problems could be summarized as follows: 1) I relied on the teleprompter too much and didn't make enough eye contact; 2) I spoke too fast (probably because I was nervous), and 3) I sometimes sounded flat and needed to put more energy into what I said via body language, be it dramatic hand gestures, facial expressions, or even punctuating certain words. Together, in our first session, we viewed the tapes and what she said was all true. Though my shortcomings made me a little glum, by the end of our time together, I was looking forward to working with Krystal and reaching my potential as a public speaker. She'd won *my* confidence.

Usually on Sundays, I wore casual sweats or an old

baggy pair of jeans and a sweatshirt. Or just lounged around in Blake's polka dot boxer shorts, which I loved to wear. But today, like Krystal, I was dressed in formal business attire—a new navy blue pantsuit and pumps—because Krystal firmly believed form equaled meaning. While I might feel more relaxed in jeans or sweats, she wanted to work with me wearing what she deemed essential for success. A powersuit. Early on in her career, she'd allowed her clients to wear casual clothes when they trained with her, but she'd noticed that when it came to doing a real-life presentation in public with more formal attire, they stiffened. And often froze. "Jennifer, you are what you wear," she told me, insisting that I invest in some designer pantsuits in time for our next session.

She was as much an image coach as she was a speech coach.

While Krystal set up the equipment for today's session, a small video camera on a tripod and a lectern, my mind drifted. I wondered how Blake was doing with Scout on his first day of obedience school. I hadn't heard from him, so I assumed no news was good news. In my heart of hearts, I knew my adorable fur baby was going to be a stellar canine student. Maybe the best in his class!

My thoughts were cut short by Krystal. "Let's begin." She ignored the bottled water I'd set on the coffee table. "Please stand behind the lectern and let me hear the short speech you've written. Pretend you're talking to an audience of five hundred. I'm going to stop you as you go along and make corrective suggestions, which I want you to implement."

I did as she asked and once behind the lectern, I cleared my throat.

"Never," Krystal snapped, "clear your throat when you may be miked or on camera. It's a sign of weakness. It shows you're nervous. And lack confidence."

I swallowed hard. She was right. I *was* nervous. And I was unnerved by her belligerence. Maybe all the sweetness she'd showed me on our first meeting was just a sugarcoated front. She was a force to be reckoned with.

"I'm sorry," I said meekly and feeling very uncomfortable in my new pantsuit. The suit didn't suit me, bad pun intended. Ordered online from Nordstrom's because of my hectic schedule, it was a little too big and frankly, I was much more comfortable in a simple A-line dress or anything my good friend Chaz Clearfield designed. I was also wearing my contact lenses rather than my glasses, which she insisted would allow me to make better eye contact with my audience and take better photographs by the press. Adding to my discomfort, they irritated my dry eyes.

Fiddling with the thick gold chain of her necklace, which was mostly hidden under the collar of her blouse, her steel-gray eyes pierced me as if apologies didn't matter. "Whatever." She glanced down at her gold watch, which must have cost a mint. "Time's awasting. Let's move on."

Over the course of the next hour, we worked on the short speech, which she'd made me prepare and memorize. "Not every venue will be able to provide a teleprompter," she'd told me, "so sometimes memory is your best and only tool." I'd written a speech about the difference between pornography and steamy romance, and why women coveted the latter. Having taken several drama classes at USC and performing in a few plays, I was good at memorization. I think it stemmed from my father, a former literature professor, who'd made me memorize verses of famous poets when I was a child. I could still recite many of them by heart.

Standing behind the lectern in my uncomfortable pantsuit and under her scrutiny, I felt stiff and nervous. The speech, which I'd rehearsed ad nauseam, began to fall apart as she criticized what seemed to be my every word and gesture.

"So *all* women want a good story and a happily ever after?" she parroted as I at last came to the end of what felt like an eternity. "You don't seem to believe a word you've written."

She was right. With all the interruptions and verbal jabs, I had no clue what I was talking about despite the fact I'd launched My Sex-TV on the premise of what women wanted.

"You choked on almost every word," she added, reaching into her leather briefcase, which she called her "bag of tricks." She slapped a sheet of paper onto the side table. "Here are some breathing exercises that I want you to practice before we meet next time so you don't sound like you're suffocating."

I was honestly exhausted by the end of the session. Drained. Walking her to the entrance to our condo, I couldn't wait to change into my sweats, take out my contacts, and relax. Read my *Los Angeles Times* and be rid of her. About to leave, she eyed the photos of Blake and me on our entryway console. There were at least a dozen, spanning from our courtship to our recent trip to Scotland. I hadn't yet added a photo of Scout, ensconced in Jeffrey's stunning silver frame.

My eyes fixed on her as she lifted one of the framed photos—that of the two of us kissing, taken at our memorable Christmas in July wedding at my parents' house this past summer—and studied it.

A smirk that seemed vaguely familiar curled on her lips. "So, that's your husband Blake." It was definitely more of a statement than a question.

"Yes. You've met him?"

She set the photo back down, her eyes still lingering on it. Her smirk morphed into a sneer, a whiff of sarcasm in her tone. "Not yet. But I'm looking forward to it."

With that, she cranked the door handle and left,

wheeling a small, efficient rollerbag that contained her practice equipment. As the heavy door closed behind her, I impulsively adjusted the photo to the exact position it had been. I was anal that way. Just like my mom. Everything in its special place.

Wistfully, I stared at the photo. Every beautiful memory of that wedding flooded my head, eradicating the malaise I felt. Blake and Scout would be home soon.

And soon, a photo of the three of us would join the many on the console.

Chapter 16
Blake

"Mmm, Jen. That feels so fucking good."

Stretched out on the bed, halfway under the covers and my eyes still glued shut, I felt her tongue lap up and down my bare chest, then stroke up and down the column of my exposed neck.

"I want you to wake me up every morning like this," I moaned as my body happily succumbed to her warm, sensuous licks. With another blissful sigh, I blindly reached out to caress her. Beneath my hand, she felt soft as velvet and I surmised she must be wearing the old velour robe she loved. The sigh gave way to a rapturous smile.

"Come here," I murmured. "Put those very pretty and talented lips of yours on mine." I felt her warm breath dust my cheeks and I inhaled through my nose. The scent of fresh coffee drifting from the kitchen was overtaken by something that smelled like oatmeal. Had my tiger made herself a bowl? It was not like her to make hot cereal on a workday morning. A toasted bagel or granola bar was more like it.

My lips still curled in a smile, I felt her very wet tongue touch down as if she was teasing me. But, that's not all that touched down. Something cold and wet did too. A sloppy slurp sounded in my ears and my eyes snapped open. Scout's head filled my entire frame of vision, his snout in my face, his tongue hanging from his mouth as if he were a lovestruck teenager.

Wiping the slobber off my face with the back of my hand, I bolted to an upright position. "Jesus, Scout. Get the fuck off!" I shouted, but the stupid dog just sat on the bed dumbfounded. "Off!" I repeated, my voice rising decibels. So much for obedience school. The fricking dog didn't budge.

My blood bubbling, I fought the urge to shove him off the bed but instead swung my legs over the side and stomped to the ensuite bathroom. Having made love to Jen in the middle of the night, I was butt naked, my cock in its normal morning wood position. Erect and at attention. To my chagrin, Scout jumped off the bed and followed me into the bathroom, getting there before I did so I was unable to close the door and keep him out. As I made my way to the toilet to do my morning business, he lowered himself onto the travertine floor beside me and just sat there, his eyes trained on me.

"Haven't you ever seen a grown man pee?" I gritted, aiming my big rigid cock at the basin and glancing his way. He cocked his head as if he were saying: "So, this is how you humans do it. You don't have to lift your leg?" With his inquisitive gaze still on me, I whizzed and relieved myself. He sure as hell wasn't taking a shower with me. Wrong. He was in the stall before I was. Loving every minute of the spraying overhead jets. "Get out, Scout!" I commanded, holding the shower door open. No luck. Ten minutes later, I was towel drying myself off. *And* my soaking wet canine companion.

When I got to the kitchen, fully dressed in a smart dark business suit and a sharp tie, Scout annoyingly trailing behind me, I found Jen, also dressed for work, sitting at the breakfast bar, her laptop in front of her. She took a sip of her coffee from her My-Sin TV mug as I strode over to the coffee maker on the counter to pour myself a cup.

"Blake, great news! I think I've solved a major problem."

"Oh. You figured out who to cast in the Nelle L'Amour series you're developing?"

"No, silly. What to do with Scout."

There was only one thing to do: get rid of him! After this morning's bed and bathroom incidents, I'd had enough. Jen would get over him. I'd buy her a diamond doggie pin—yup, that would do it. Easy peasy. Grinning at what a genius I was, I headed to the fridge to add some cream. My back was to my wife as she rambled on.

"We can't leave him here all day, baby, while we're at work."

True.

"And we can't leave him on the terrace. It's still not dog-proofed."

True.

"We don't really know our neighbors so we can't ask them to look after him or walk him."

True.

"And I spoke to both the concierge and doorman, and they're unable to leave their posts."

So . . .

"I've found a . . ."

Balls! She found a dog walker! Some nearby, money-hungry UCLA student to check in on Scout and take him out.

" . . . doggy daycare center."

What!?? Holding my mug of piping hot coffee, I joined my tiger at the breakfast bar. Scout lying down contently on the floor beside her. Her bespectacled eyes were still glued to her computer screen. Though I felt a little slighted, I couldn't help noticing how cute she looked in her tortoise-rimmed glasses. Somehow, her sexy librarian look made her sexier. More fuckable. Did we have time for a quickie before we went to work? I nuzzled her neck to get her aroused, but the only thing that seemed to excite her was the damn computer screen.

"Blake, listen to this. '*Four Paws Only.* A twenty-four hour facility offering large indoor and outdoor spaces for your fur baby to play and socialize in while in our loving care. Large dogs and small dogs are separated under the watch of our carefully trained staff and enjoy a variety of activities, including exercise ramps, games, and supervised walks throughout the day. We know some fur babies suffer from separation anxiety, so we offer curbside service and meet you right at the drop off. There's no need to even leave your car! Just be sure to bring their favorite food and snacks so they don't get hungry. We guarantee that your dog will be wanting to come back for more or your money back guaranteed!'"

Pausing, Jen clicked on the photos tab.

While I looked on in silence, Jen jabbed the montage of photos, one after another of happy dogs, all different sizes and breeds, climbing up and down ramps, dashing around the spacious facility with chew toys, and playing with other dogs as well as with the staff. Jen's voice grew more excited. "Blake, doesn't this place look awesome—it's like a playgroup for dogs—and it's located in Culver City close to our offices! It's perfect for Scout! For us! Don't you think so too?"

She had to be kidding. My mind raced. I had to talk her out of this and convince her the only place we should take Scout was back to the pound. He needed a home with a yard and someone who was readily available to feed and walk him. "Jen, I don't think this is a good idea at all. We don't know how socialized Scout is."

"But you told me he did so well in obedience school yesterday! And even made friends with that pit bull!"

I had told Jen all about our obedience school experience, boasting that Scout had done great, not wanting to admit failure to myself. That dictator instructor implying I was weak and befuddled. Screw her! I'd also relayed the unexpected Katrina incident, which my tiger had found hysterically funny. And led her to give Scout a special treat for his extraordinary behavior. Damn! I needed to come up with a different tactic. *Think, genius. Think.* And being the true genius I was, it came to me fast.

"Jen, this place is probably a scam. They're not showing us the photos of dogs attacking each other. Or sharing testimonies of people who had terrible experiences—like their dogs getting bit or coming down with fatal diseases. They just want our money!"

"Blake, they're offering the first two days free! And I read all the Yelp reviews. There wasn't one under four stars! Everyone raved about this place!" She cast her eyes down at the beast. "Scout, sweetie, don't you want to go to doggy daycare?"

The dog clambered to a sitting position, looking up to her with his loving eyes and eagerly thumping his tail against the floor.

"Look, Blake! He understood! He wants to go!"

Thump, thump, thump, thump.

Fuck, fuck, fuck, fuck.

There wasn't anything I could say or do to dissuade her. Fuck me. Armed with his choke chain, Scout was out the door before we were.

~~~

My day at work couldn't have been better. I closed two major deals that would infuse a shitload of money into Conquest Broadcasting. And I got our quarterly ratings report. They were at an all time high. All divisions. And much to my pleasure, Jen's My Sin-TV was showing the most growth. Her visionary erotic women's channel was proving to be a cash cow. My incredible wife deserved to be taken out for a surprise dinner at The Palm to celebrate over lobsters and champagne, but just as I was about to buzz my longtime secretary Mrs. Cho to make a reservation, my office phone rang. The phone flashed red, the special hotline I'd set up for my tiger, so her calls could bypass Mrs. Cho and come directly to me. My dick twitched beneath my desk. Maybe she was horny and had the time for a mid afternoon tryst. Banging her over my desk was one of my favorite pastimes.

I picked up, putting the call on speaker. "Hi, babe.

What's up?" I could answer that question myself. My dick! It was fully erect, ready for action.

"Blake, there's been an incident with Scout." Her voice sounded panicked. "We have to go to the doggy daycare center right away!"

As fast as Mr. Burns rose to attention, he deflated.

Fuck. This. Dog.

Chapter 17
Blake

The doggy daycare center was a five-minute drive from Conquest Broadcasting, located on Main Street in Culver City. We took my car which we'd driven in together to the office, something we did often when neither of us had an outside meeting. After circling the block twice, we found a metered parking spot right outside the facility. Without acknowledging the half-dozen dogs lined up against the front window who eyed us with various degrees of curiosity, friendliness, and suspicion, we hurried inside, me holding Jen's hand which was cold as ice. Waiting for an attendant, we surveyed the place, searching for Scout. The play area was spacious, with a plexiglass divider separating small dogs from large ones. Accompanied by staff members, the rambunctious dogs were engaged in various activities from climbing up and down assorted sized ramps to playing with various chew toys. Cacophonous barking and scampering filled the air, which smelled of disinfectant. Nausea rising to my chest, not to mention the beginnings of a splitting headache, I wanted to get out of this place as fast I could.

Jen squeezed my hand. "I don't see Scout anywhere!"

"Maybe he's in the play yard outside or they took him for a walk."

"Blake, maybe something terrible happened to him!"

Before I could reassure her that he was fine—he probably just had an "accident"—a tall, skinny girl with a shock of spiky pink hair, nose piercings, and an armful of tattoos, moseyed up to us. She hadn't been here in the morning when we dropped Scout off.

"Can I help you?" she drawled, thrusting her bony hip. She looked and sounded like she was stoned. Hey, I'd be stoned, too, if I had to work in this joint.

"We're here for our dog Scout," responded Jen, her voice anxious. "Someone called us and said there was some kind of 'incident.'"

"Hmm. I'm not sure what happened. I just started my shift. Let me call my supervisor."

Jen's eyes stayed glued on her as she reached for a pager that was clipped to the waistband of her ripped jeans.

"Glinda, I have a couple here who are looking for their dog Scout."

"I'll be right there." The voice was curt. And husky.

A few moments later, Glinda joined us. She definitely bore no resemblance to the Good Witch of the North, whom I had a secret crush on as a kid. I swear every time I watched the *Wizard of Oz*, my eight-year-old self got a woody when the beautiful, princessy strawberry blond waved her magic wand and sang, "Come out, come out wherever you are."

This woman was no beauty. The shaved-head, buxom broad wore baggy khaki pants and an ill-fitting T-shirt. With her jowly face and stout physique, she reminded me of a bulldog.

"Hi," said Jen meekly. "We're Mr. and Mrs. Burns. Is our dog Scout all right?"

Without as much as a hello, Glinda got straight to the point. "I'm sorry to say that Scout can no longer come here."

My tiger's angst-filled expression grew confused. "So, he's okay?"

"He's fine. However, he bit another dog, which is totally unacceptable. We have him confined in lockup."

"What! That's not possible! Scout's the sweetest dog ever!" My wife turned to me, her eyes pleading for support. "Blake, tell her! Tell her that Scout's the best dog ever!"

Seriously? The fricking dog had destroyed half our house, devoured fine jewelry, and almost flunked out of obedience school. And that was just in the last forty-eight hours.

"Um, uh, can you possibly show us the dog he bit?"

Glinda scowled. "Very well. Follow me."

We followed her to the "large dog" section. All the dogs looked twice the size of Scout I observed as she pointed to the dog Scout had allegedly attacked.

Otto.

A sleek, ninety-pound Doberman Pinscher, his ears cropped and his tail docked. Call me prejudiced, but I hated Dobermans. And so did my parents and Grandma. When my sister Marcy and I were kids, they'd ingrained in us they were Nazi dogs. Extremely vicious and out for Jews. Not believing them, I changed my mind when the Dobie of our Beverly Hills neighbor, a German industrialist, broke loose from his yard and attacked my Hebrew teacher.

With Jen by my side, I stared at the dog and he stared back at me with a snarl. His razor-sharp fangs showing. His hackles bristling. *Enemy detected.* My nerves buzzing, I tried to keep my cool as the words of Glinda the Wicked Bitch drifted into my ears.

"Otto is one of our longest, most beloved clients. His owners, the Von Schmidts, are major benefactors. If anything ever happened to him, we would shut down."

Yup, it all boiled down to money. To be honest, I doubted that Scout had aggressively attacked this vicious Satan-horned beast. It was probably the other way around and Scout had bit him in self-defense. But there was no point in defending him as I couldn't prove a thing. And besides, whose side was Fraulein Glinda going to take? Former Gestapo dog's or former bar mitzvah boy's?

"Is Otto going to be okay?" I asked, secretly hoping the dog would contract some rare fatal disease and rot in hell.

"Our in-house medical technician examined him and doesn't think he'll need any stitches."

"That's good," mumbled a stunned Jen.

"But if he does get an infection and this unfortunate incident leads to a lawsuit, our contract spells out that you are responsible."

"No problem." My posture grew stiff, my hands fisting by my sides so I wouldn't shake the shit out of this woman. "Now, can we please have our dog?"

"Fine." She slapped back the word and then asked the pink-haired stonehead to retrieve him.

Five minutes—and one steaming turd—later, we were out the door. My tiger elated. And our dog equally excited to get the hell out of this shithole and go home. Much to his credit, he'd left a souvenir.

It seemed ridiculous to go back to work. It was already three o'clock in the afternoon and neither of us had anything pressing on our schedules. Plus, we had no place to leave Scout who could not be left unattended. So we headed home.

Before taking the elevator up to our condo, we gave him a short walk down Wilshire and to our relief, he conked out in his bed upon our return.

"He's so cute," cooed Jen, glancing down at his curled up body.

I am, too, I silently retorted.

"I can't believe he'd bite a soul. That mean looking dog must have instigated him." A pause. "Blake, what if the owners sue us and try to take *our* Scout away?"

I weighed the possibilities. And the word "our." Maybe the incident was a mixed blessing in disguise. The Von Schmidts, who didn't need the money, might drop their lawsuit if we got rid of Scout. I would agree to send him to a dog farm in the Midwest. Give a hefty donation to the doggie concentration camp and wipe my hands clean and free of the beast once and for all.

"Jen, it's all going to be okay," I reassured her, wrapping an arm around her slender shoulders. "Let's not worry about what might *not* happen."

"But—"

"But what, baby?" Not giving her a chance to respond, I gathered her in my arms and walked her backward into the ensuite bathroom. "C'mon, let's take a relaxing bath."

My idea of relaxing might be different than yours. For me, it meant soaking in our Jacuzzi tub with my tiger in my arms, her back against my chest, my cock buried between her legs. The steamy bubbling water gurgled as I pumped my tiger in this position, my hands cupping and massaging her dainty breasts in tandem. Her head tilting back, her back arching, her hands gripping my thighs, she met my thrusts with little breathy bounces.

"Oh God Blake, I really needed this."

"Tell me, baby."

"Do you think Scout was traumatized by his doggie daycare experience?"

I mentally growled. The mention of Scout almost broke my concentration. Bringing my tiger and myself to a stratospheric climax took a lot of determination. And a lot of focus. Seriously, how could she be thinking of that damn dog when I was banging her with such force? All I could think about was making her fall apart all around me, my own epic orgasm chasing hers. And all she should be thinking about was yours fucking truly.

"Tiger, stop worrying about him. He's fine. Stay in the moment."

I moved my hands to her haunches, gripping them, as I picked up my pace. Pumping her harder. Faster. Bringing us closer to the edge.

Just as I expected, she quieted, except for those delightful whimpers, which harmonized with my guttural grunts. I was so close to combusting I couldn't take it anymore.

"Come for me, baby," I urged, moving one hand to her clit, rubbing it to ecstasy.

"Oh, Blake!" Her body shuddered against mine as my cock exploded inside her.

Mission accomplished.

All squeaky clean and sexed out (in other words, relaxed), Jen and I retreated to our bedroom. We were wearing our matching terrycloth robes, one belt loop away from another round of screwing. I was looking forward to making love in our freshly refurbished bed. Jen and I had made a trip to Bed Bath & Beyond yesterday afternoon to replace all the bedding Scout destroyed. All of it top of the line and yummy. My cock hardening, I stepped foot inside and my eyes bugged out.

Big mistake! We'd accidentally left the bedroom door open.

One of us was humping, but it wasn't me!

Chapter 18
Blake

Holy Moses!

My bulging eyes zoomed in on our bed.

I couldn't believe it. Scout was on it. This time *not* destroying our new pillows and comforter. A new activity!

Our dog was humping Jen's oversized plush white tiger! The only stuffed thing on our bed that had survived his Saturday night rampage. There was a reason. And it was now obvious.

Scout was in love with *his* tiger as much as I was with mine.

"Oh my God, Blake, what's he doing?"

"I think he's found a friend with benefits," I muttered as he pounded the stuffed animal with unbridled determination. Oblivious to us. Finally, he slowed down and pulled away.

And then Jen let out a frantic shriek that pierced my ears. Her hand flew to her mouth.

"Oh my God, Blake! Look!" With her other hand,

she pointed to the long, thick shiny red *thing* dangling between his legs. "His guts are coming out!"

I followed her gaze. Holy shit!

"What is that?" Her voice was a shaky mix of fright and repulsion.

"His thingie!"

"His thingie? What do you mean?"

"His wiener." It looked just like one of those jumbo Hebrew National hot dogs my grandma liked to grill.

"Blake, but he's fixed. Something's very wrong with him! He looks like he's in pain! And why isn't it going away?"

Five minutes later we were on our way to Dr. Chase's new office, Scout in the car, still fully erect.

Dr. Chase's new office was located in Culver City in a non-descript strip mall on Santa Monica Boulevard, not far from our condo. Though on the small side, it was sleek and modern, with black leather seating and interesting black and white wildlife photos artistically placed on the walls in the reception area. Despite his condition, Scout was in rare form, hyperactively panting and sniffing everything in sight. Praying to God he wouldn't take a dump, I held him tightly by his leash to keep him away from the scowling woman with a puff of white hair, who was guarding her caged, frightened cat. The cat's mewling was getting under my skin. I wanted to stuff a sock in its mouth. Then, to make matters worse, Scout began to bark at him.

"Can't you control your animal?" the woman snapped as Jen made her way to the receptionist.

The receptionist's face was obscured by her desktop computer, but upon hearing the commotion Scout was causing, she looked up. I recognized her instantly. And so did Jen. And so did an excited Scout, whose barking morphed into a gleeful howl. It was Tessa, the girl from the dog shelter, who'd introduced us to Scout. Her eyes lit up at the sight of us and then she sprung up from her chair and came around the console to hug Jen.

"Jen! It's so good to see you again! And thank you so much for the recommendation! I just love working with Dr. Chase, and I've already learned so much in a single day."

"I'm so happy for you," replied my beautiful wife, a smile lifting her lips for the first time since we had sex this afternoon.

Tessa squatted down and hugged Scout, giving him a big, juicy kiss on the top of his head. "Hi, handsome boy! What brings you here?"

Wagging his tail vigorously, our dog licked her face. I was feeling very left out. All this love and praise for this canine beast that had only cost us problems. And thousands of dollars. Raising my voice above the still mewling cat, I responded.

"Um, er, he has a big problem." Shelter Girl followed my gaze. "He had a little tryst and it won't go down."

Now sitting, Scout's erection was very obvious. At the sight of his boner, Shelter Girl's eyes widened while Cat Lady gave both him and me a disgusted look. Now, after all the kisses and affection, poor Scout didn't seem too happy. Uncomfortable and embarrassed was more like it. And possibly in pain. He let out a whimper. To my surprise, my heart felt for him. A connection. I knew what this was like, having suffered a frightening bout of life-threatening priapism a month earlier. Well, it wasn't really life threatening, but it sure felt like it then. As much as I despised this pain-in-the-ass dog, panic set in.

"Tessa," I spat out, "this is an emergency. Can Dr. Chase see Scout right away?"

"Please!" begged Jen.

Tessa hurried back to her desk and picked up her phone.

One minute later, a technician came out and led us back to Dr. Chase's examination quarters. Cat Lady looked like she wanted to claw me.

"Thanks for seeing us on such short notice," said Jen with a small grateful smile as we piled into the small, sterile examining room.

"No, problem," replied Dr. Chase, dressed much like before in jeans, a Scooby-Doo T-shirt, sneakers, and a white lab jacket. "And thank you for introducing me to Tessa. We've had a busy first day and she's been doing an amazing job. She told me she wants to be a veterinarian and I hope she'll get plenty of pre-vet school training here." He circled around Scout, not looking very alarmed, and then his eyes flitted to me. "So, you got your unicorn pin back?"

"Yeah, it's better than new."

"Great. And no rectum problems? Like blood in his stool?"

"No, nothing like that. But we have a new problem that's freaking us out."

He followed my gaze. Scout's dangling crimson wiener was hard to miss. It stuck out like a sore thumb, no pun intended.

"Ah, I see what the problem is. Paraphimosis."

"Paraphimosis?" Jen repeated, her voice shaky.

"Yes, the technical term for a male dog's inability to retract his penis back into his prepuce—aka his sheath." He squatted down and planted his hands on Scout's flanks. "So buddy, did you have a little fling? A brunette like your mama?"

Scout cocked his head. I cocked my brow and bristled. Any physical reference to my tiger by this movie star handsome vet incensed me. "Actually it was with one of my wife's stuffed animals."

Chasehole chuckled. "That's common too."

"But doc, his balls are chopped off. How's that possible?"

"Even after they're fixed, many male dogs still have a lot of pent up sexual energy and they need to release it."

"Is it fixable?" Jen asked nervously. "I mean, can you treat the problem?"

"Yes, it's DIY. You can do it at home. But's it's a good thing you brought him in. Extended paraphimosis can cause the penis to become extremely dry and painful, often interfering with the proper flow of urine, and lead to major bladder problems."

Gah! A shiver skittered down my spine and my cock twitched. I never thought I could have so much empathy for this stupid canine creature as we watched the vet apply some lubricant to his exposed wiener and gently massage it back into its sheath.

"Bingo!" he shouted as Scout's manhood fully retracted. "All better."

"Is that all we have to do?"

"Yup. It's as simple as that. Any cream or moisturizer will do. Dermadoo is especially good if you can find some."

At the mention of the D-word, a pain shot through my cock. After my own form of paraphi-whatever which may have been caused by that cream, I never wanted to go near the stuff again. N-E-V-E-R. Not wanting to share my nightmarish experience with Chasehole or find out if he'd ever used it, I shakily asked, "Can you recommend anything else?"

"K-Y Jelly is also really good."

"Ooh, we have lots of that at home!" chirped Jen.

I cringed, feeling something between mortified and violated. Well, I guess we were going to have to share my tiger's vibrator jelly with the fricking dog. We'd better order a case.

Putting the cap back on the tube of lubricant, Chasehole added that we could also use a cold compress. It worked well too.

"So, how can we prevent this from happening again? Can we teach him not to hump things in obedience school?" As an aside, I quickly told the doctor that I'd enrolled Scout in the obedience school he'd recommended and then lied through my teeth that he was a stellar pupil.

Chasehole laughed. "I'm afraid not. You'll need to hide that tiger or put it some place where Scout can't reach it." He bent down and affectionately patted the dog's head. "What he needs is a big yard to run around in to release all his pent up sexual energy."

When we got home, Jen's plush tiger was sitting on top of our tall armoire out of Scout's reach and at *my* tiger's insistence, I was on the phone again with my mother.

Chapter 19
Blake

A week passed, then another, then a month. It was hard to believe it was the beginning of December. Our official first anniversary, my thirty-first birthday, which happened to fall on the same day, and the holidays were around the corner. And Scout would be with us to celebrate each of these monumental occasions.

We'd gotten into a routine with Scout. Every morning, Jen and I got up early and went on a long walk with him. Then we fed him and got ready for work before dropping him off at my parents' house. It was Jen's bright idea after the Hebrew National incident to call my mother and ask if Scout could stay there on weekdays while we worked. And until we bought a house with a yard. Though I didn't want to resort to my mother's help yet again, it panned out much to my surprise. And relief.

Scout loved hanging out in my parents' backyard. There were acres to explore and lots of rabbits, birds, and squirrels to chase after to keep him amused. The highlight of his day was taking a swim in the Olympic-size pool, which no one ever used. My mother preferred to play tennis with her cronies, and my father, golf. In no time, Scout became best friends with the gardeners, the pool guy, and all the other staffers.

Despite all his activities, he started to put on some weight thanks to the delicious meals my grandma, who lived in the guesthouse, made for him and the treats she sneaked him. I mean, how many dogs got fed pastrami on rye with a side of slaw? Or cream cheese rugelach in the mid afternoon? The crazy dog loved to eat everything! Plus, he got to stay at my parents' house every Friday for Shabbat, much to my eight-year-old twin nephews' delight, and consume all the brisket leftovers.

"Chow *shmow!*" declared my indulgent grandma. Even my mother, who never fed her designer pooches dog food, contributed.

Each day, Scout's behavior improved. He heeled when I walked him and was a pro at the commands: SIT, STAY, LAY DOWN, and COME. And he no longer chewed up things . . . well mostly. Much to my pride, he graduated from the Royal Canine Obedience School, coming in second in his class right after Boyd's Attila. Plus, he got another ribbon for being "Most Improved Student." Drill sergeant Martha, whom I'd grown to respect, gave me one too. And a hug.

There was still, however, one big problem: my

award-winning black Lab mix still did not seem to grasp one simple two-letter word: NO.

—NO, Scout. Off the couch!

—NO, Scout. Get your paws off the dining table.

—NO, Scout. You cannot rummage through the garbage.

—NO, Scout. You cannot chew on my nine hundred dollar handmade Italian loafers.

—NO, Scout. You cannot chew up my rare Cuban cigars.

—NO, Scout. You cannot come up on the bed unless we call for you.

—NO, Scout. You cannot sniff Jen's crotch.

—NO, Scout. You cannot play with Jen's underwear.

The latter was particularly a problem. He would steal Jen's panties whenever he could, especially when our housekeeper Blanca had them in the laundry basket and wasn't looking. Just as I would settle into my favorite chair to watch a little TV after dinner, he'd bring me a pair, dangling from his jaw, and I'd try to wrestle them away from him. I suppose it was my fault it became a game—a game of tug of war. A battle of will and might. Unfortunately, my strength was no match for his strong canine jaw, and Jen's flimsy G-strings usually ended up in shreds. She thought it was laugh-out-loud funny and reminded me that she had a limitless supply of sexy underwear from Gloria's

Secret, thanks to making a mutually lucrative My Sin-TV sponsorship deal with CEO Gloria Long Zander, the wife of my best bud, Jaime.

Thank fuck, sex with Jen was never a problem. It couldn't have been better. Scout had his own tiger—his stuffed animal with benefits—which we let him have access to, now that we knew how to fix his potential issue. While Jen and I fucked our brains out, Scout "played" with his "friend," as we called him. It was a win-win for everyone. Although I'm not sure what the toy tiger got out of it except a lot of wear and tear.

This holiday season we had a lot to celebrate. The jeweled unicorn I'd bought Jen in Scotland had brought us luck. We were having a baby! Yes! In July!

Thanks to my sister Marcy. Marcy, an esteemed OB-GYN, who'd been the one to share the great news that Jen, despite her hysterectomy, could still produce eggs because she still had one functioning ovary. However, because her uterus had been partially removed, she was unable to carry a child and hence we would need to find a surrogate. We'd begun the search for one as soon as we heard that exciting news back in February, but our search had been challenging. California was one of the few places in the world where surrogacy was sanctioned, and hence demand was much greater than supply, with infertile couples, gay couples, and couples in our situation being put on long wait lists. It was unlikely we'd be introduced to a suitable surrogate for over a year regardless of how much money we offered. Money couldn't buy us a child. Our disappointment and frustration could fill volumes.

When Marcy learned about this disheartening situation, she did something we never dreamed of. Something so selfless, so loving I owed her forever. She offered to try to get impregnated with Jen's fertilized eggs and carry our baby. Though she was almost forty, she was in excellent physical health and her hormone levels were comparable to those of a twenty-year old—which made me think that my newly divorced sister must be horny as hell. Just to assure us (and likely herself too), she had another trusted gynecologist substantiate her fitness and ability to carry a child to term. Not only could she carry a child, but with her brick house uterus, she was still capable of carrying twins.

Throughout September, we'd gone through fertility treatments to maximize the quality and quantity of Jen's eggs. She produced three, all A+ and in a petri dish, after jerking off, I fertilized all of them. Mr. Burns's sperm were not only swimmers; they were Olympic champions. Two of the embryos were transplanted into Marcy's uterus, the other frozen for the future. Needless to say, my tiger and I were nervous Nellies, the timely trip to Scotland somewhat easing our anxiety. Exactly one month to the day after we got Scout, Marcy called us to tell us some news. She was pregnant! And on that afternoon, we all went on an outing to celebrate and to look at houses. In nine months, Scout would have his own yard, and we'd have a baby! To not jinx things, we mutually agreed that we wouldn't tell all our friends and family members the exciting news until Christmas Day. Our special gift to each and every one.

Life was good! Work was good! Sex was good! And it was all only going to get better. Both Jen and I couldn't wait for the new addition to our family. Any fears we had about Scout being jealous of the baby, be it a boy or girl (we wanted to be surprised) or being a danger were assuaged by our visits to Jaime and Gloria and their twins, Payton and Pauline, at their Malibu beach house.

More than anything, Scout loved the beach. It was a joy to watch him romp in the waves and race across the sand, chasing squawking seagulls. But what gave both Jen and me the most happiness was watching him interact with the rambunctious twins, who were in the midst of their terrible twos. No matter what they did to him—be it pull his tail, try to ride him, or throw a handful of sand at him—he remained calm. It was obvious he understood they did not mean harm. And when he played catch with them with his chewed up tennis ball and lay down protectively by their side during naps, it was even more obvious he adored them. Scout was not just good with kids; he was great with them. He'd passed that test with flying colors.

And then the next big test came. I was going away on a weeklong business trip to Las Vegas for the National Association of Broadcaster's Digital Conference, where I'd see many of our affiliate managers from around the country, including my favorite, Vera Nichols, who headed up our very profitable Vegas station.

"Come with me, tiger," I insisted, "even for a couple days. Vera and her husband would love to see you and have us to their house for dinner."

Fresh from our morning shower together (and our morning quickie), Jen in her fluffy robe, stood before the bathroom mirror blow drying her wet, shoulder-length chestnut hair. Scout, as usual, was seated on the floor beside her, barking wildly at the dryer as if it were some kind of foe. Much like my parents' gardeners' leaf blowers, it drove him crazy.

"Baby, I wish I could," she shouted, making herself heard above the loud hum of the hairdryer and Scout's woofs. "But I can't. We're behind. We have to wrap up post-production on Lauren Blakely's *Well Hung*, and I have some important authors flying in from the UK to pitch their books." A pause. "Plus, I have my final public speaking class on Sunday."

My tiger hadn't talked much about the latter for whatever reason. I supposed the sessions were going well though I hadn't asked. Standing next to her, a towel wrapped around my waist, I applied some product into my already blown hair while I looked at myself in the mirror. Man, I was handsome. I had to admit it. Even when a frown tugged at my lips.

"C'mon, baby. You can move a few things around."

I heard her sigh as she switched off the blow dryer, and Scout calmed down. "Honestly, Blake, I can't." Grabbing an elastic band, she swept her hair up into a high ponytail. "It involves too many people and with the holidays coming, everyone wants to wrap things up so they can take time off."

My lips twitched with resignation. And disappointment. I had been looking forward to going to Vegas with my tiger, and at first when I mentioned the trip, she thought she could come with me—if all went to schedule. Sin City was a special place for us . . . the city where I first realized I was madly in love with her. I'd followed her there on a business trip, but business had turned into pleasure. And something much more the night I held her in my arms and we slow-danced to a lounge singer's rendition of "The First Time Ever I Saw Your Face." Our forever song. The fond memory spun in my head, but in lieu of a smile, a frustrated breath blew out of my mouth. Admittedly, I understood Jen's decision. As the head of My Sex-TV, my tiger had both responsibilities and deadlines, and she didn't take them lightly. And of course, things didn't stay on schedule. They never did. The female lead of the steamy telenovela had come down with the flu so production had to be halted for a week. Then, the male lead, whom she'd kissed over and over in retakes, got it too. Yet another week of delays.

From the day I met Jen, what could go wrong would go wrong. So, was our pattern. Somehow, we always triumphed over adversity and came out stronger.

A small consolation. I heaved another breath of resignation. I had no choice. I was going to Vegas by myself.

I really hated leaving my wife alone, especially now that she was going to be the mother of my child. *Our* child. Usually, when I went away on a business trip, she stayed with Libby or her BFF came over. But this time Libby was away on a business trip and then was going to visit her boyfriend Everett in France. We still hadn't hooked her up with Chasehole, because she was, as she put it, "unavailable."

"Jen, why don't you stay with Chaz and Jeffrey? They'll let you bring Scout. Or how about my parents?"

No matter how hard I tried to convince her, my tiger out-and-out refused. Even my two last-ditch efforts failed. "Baby, aren't you going to be so lonely here without me?" Followed by: "Aren't you going to be scared staying here all by yourself?" "Blake," she retorted as she applied a light coat of mascara to her already long, thick eyelashes, "we live in a high-security building where there's never been a problem, and plus now we have Scout. I'll be here for him, and he'll be here for me."

I let it go. For the first time since we'd gotten Scout, Jen would be staying in the condo alone without me. It was a chance to test Scout's mettle—to revisit the reason we got him in the first place. To be Jen's protector.

I wasn't sure. Doubt crept into my bones as my departure date crept closer.

Three days later, my bags were packed. After a glorious night of passionate lovemaking, I kissed my still-in-bed wife good-bye.

"I love you, baby. Stay safe. I'll be back at the end of the week, but I'll call you every chance I have." Not telling her that I planned to have Skype sex with her nightly, I kissed her again, and she let out a groggy, contented moan. "I love you too. Have a safe trip and give Vera and Steve—and their son Josh—a big hug from me."

As she closed her eyes to grab another short half-hour of sleep, I tiptoed out of the room with my luggage, Scout trotting behind me.

I fed our ravenous dog before I made my way to the airport for my seven a.m. flight.

"Take good care of her, boy!" Bending down, I scratched him behind his ears, a favorite spot.

He looked up to me with those big brown puppy eyes, and stared at me earnestly. Wagging his tail as if he were saying, "I promise. Scout's honor."

I gave him the three-finger salute and then was out the door.

Chapter 20
Jennifer

The doorbell rang. Jetting to the door before I could get there in my heels, Scout barked madly. The bell was a trigger for his sometimes manic behavior. He barked anytime someone rang the bell or knocked, except for Blake's grandma whose scrumptious homemade food he could smell from the second she stepped out of the elevator. When Grandma came by, he squealed and his tail wagged into a blur. For all others, he was almost rabid, showing his fangs with non-stop snarls, growls, and woofs.

The bell rang again. I knew who it was. Krystal Clare. My public speaking coach, who was here for our last and final Sunday session. With Blake still away in Vegas on a business trip, it was the first time Scout was home with me at this time instead of being in obedience school or on a long walk with him.

"Scout," I admonished, stumbling to the door in my high heels and stiff business attire, which Krystal still insisted I wear. "Calm down. Stop barking. It's someone I work with."

Nothing I could do or say could calm him down. Holding him back by his leather collar (he never wore his choke chain in the house), I managed to crank open the door halfway. Scout almost managed to get out, startling my instructor. His growl and her shriek collided in my ears. She flinched, jumping back a foot.

"Oh my God! Put that beast away! I hate dogs!"

I held Scout back with all my might as he continued to growl. Ready to attack. I'd never seen such a vehement reaction to anyone at the door.

"Bad!" I yelled at my beloved dog, my sharp tone stabbing me with guilt.

Scout ignored my one word though he knew it well. Blake had used it numerous times when he stole my underwear and even I had when he'd rummaged through the garbage and left a total mess on the kitchen floor. And on the occasional time he peed or pooped in the house.

"Krystal, I'm so sorry. He doesn't know you."

"I don't give a damn! Get him away from me! Now!" Her harsh voice was nothing like I'd ever heard before. Though it reeked of fear, it felt more like a threat.

With all the muscle power I could muster, I dragged Scout into our bedroom, closing the door behind me after promising him a treat for good behavior. When I returned, Krystal had let herself into the condo and was setting up her equipment. We'd covered a lot of ground. Reciting a speech from memory. Communicating with a mic in my hand. Responding to interview questions, be it prepared ones or impromptu. Presenting a PowerPoint. And reading off a teleprompter. Today, I was going to practice one last and final time with a teleprompter, delivering a speech I'd prepared.

With Scout still yelping in the bedroom, I took my place behind the lectern while Krystal settled into her usual chair to observe me. The video camera, perched on a tripod next to her, was aimed at me, and in front of me was a portable teleprompter.

"Begin," ordered Krystal with a clap of her hands. Over the course of my sessions with her, she'd grown more demanding. And short-tempered. And instead of growing more confident with my public speaking skills, I'd grown more insecure. She'd criticized and berated me. Rarely complimenting me to make me feel good. As much as I wanted to, I didn't tell Blake. He'd courageously made it through Scout's obedience school with drill sergeant Martha, and the two of them had graduated with flying colors. If they could do it, I could do it. Make it through Krystal Clare's public speaking course and prove to both Blake and his father that I had what it took to bring My Sin-TV to the next level.

My gaze stayed on Krystal as she crossed one ankle over the other and folded her hands on her lap. Today, she was wearing a white pantsuit with a Christmas-red blouse and red-soled pumps. Her monogrammed briefcase was on the floor beside her within an arm's reach. Her eyes bored into mine. Anxiously, I fiddled with Blake's beautiful unicorn pin, which I'd pinned on the lapel of my jacket for good luck.

"What are you waiting for?" she snapped. "The teleprompter is loaded."

I refrained from clearing my throat and gazed at the two screens in front of me. Half of the speech I'd prepared would appear on the right one, half on the left one, the lines alternating. Though one would think reading from a teleprompter would be a breeze and make speech-giving way easier, it was actually challenging. You had to seamlessly shift your vision from one screen to the other while maintaining eye contact with your audience, tricking those who were watching into thinking you knew your speech by heart. The final speech that Krystal had asked me to write had been a challenging one. One that tested my courage and emotions. It was an imaginary farewell address to Conquest Broadcasting. A good-bye to my job as the head of My Sin-TV. Ready to start, I focused on the right teleprompter.

"I have a confession. A *big* one. When I came to Conquest Broadcasting, I had *no* idea what this job would entail. I did not know that it would dramatically change my life. And *completely* change that of others."

So far, so good. I spoke slowly and clearly with

conviction, pausing for dramatic effect and punching certain words to sound dynamic. And throwing in a smile for good measure. Feeling secure, I subtly shifted my eyes to the left screen as the next lines of my speech popped up.

"I did something unforgiveable."

Wait! Something's wrong. I wrote *unimaginable.* It must be an error. Some kind of autocorrect thing. I paused as confusion washed over me.

"Continue!" ordered Krystal. "I don't have all day."

With an uncomfortable feeling looming in the pit of my stomach, I resumed. Except my mouth went dry as I read the next line, unable to get the words out.

I cost an innocent man, not only his job, but also his life.

"Speak up, Jennifer," hissed Krystal. "I can't hear you."

Facing her, I blinked hard. My heartbeat sped up. "This is not what I wrote."

Krystal snorted. "Of course you didn't. I did!"

My eyes stayed fixated on her. I could feel the blood draining from my face, my pulse pounding in my ears as I silently read the next lines.

No, he didn't deserve to be fired from his job. Lose the career he'd worked his ass off for. Or to be brutally murdered.

My head spinning, I couldn't go on. I looked at the woman sitting before me straight in the eye. "Who are you?"

Scout's relentless woofs clogged my ears as my heart thudded awaiting her response.

A slow, wicked smile slithered across her face. "Duh! Krystal Clare." Then a beat. "Maybe I should *clar*ify?" She put air quotes around the last word, emphasizing the first syllable. My stomach lurched in anticipation.

"Krystal Clare," she repeated and then the shocker. "Springer."

The surname sliced through the fog of my brain like a bolt of lightning and a paralyzing electric current ran down my spine. My legs turning to jelly, my bones to liquid, I gripped the edges of the lectern for support. "You're Don Springer's wife?" I stammered.

She rolled her eyes and smirked. That familiar smirk that had tugged at my brain, week after week. No, she wasn't his wife.

The telling smirk morphed into a more telling snarl. "I'm his sister, you stupid bitch. And *you* killed my brother!"

My lips quivered and every muscle in my body shook as the words sunk in. It took me several moments to reply. "I didn't kill your brother!"

"Bullshit!"

The nightmarish events of that life-changing night whirled around in my mind like a maelstrom. Unbeknownst to me, the deranged game show producer had broken out of the Vegas prison where he was being held for assault and made his way to the house I shared with my best friend Libby, who wasn't home. His tight, suffocating grip around my neck... my escape from him on my crutches... his ruthless pursuit... my struggle on the floor as he tried to rape me... then kill me with his knife and he would have if Blake hadn't shown up in the nick of time. The image of Blake stabbing Springer with my crutch over and over until all life ebbed out of him played on a loop in my head.

"My husband did! He saved me from being killed by the bastard!"

"How dare you call my brother a bastard?"

"He was! A *sick* bastard! A rapist!" Actually no one other than Blake knew that. Springer had almost raped me when I was in college and then again while I was overseeing his perverted game show, *Wheel of Pain*, which Blake, my hero, circumvented before firing him. To protect me, we'd kept his sexual assaults out of the news and spun the final chapter of the story into a botched up robbery attempt, the motive revenge, with Blake killing him in self-defense. His body was autopsied and then cremated. Blake and I moved on, never knowing he had a next of kin.

Krystal's eyes flooded with fury, her face turning as screaming red as her blouse. "I don't believe you!"

"It's the truth, Krystal. Your brother engaged in sexual violence. He got off on hurting women. Emotionally and physically. I wasn't the only victim. Just the lucky one who got away." *Twice.*

She glowered at me, a crease forming between her tightly knitted brows, a dark cloud of bitterness falling over her face. "It wasn't his fault! Our mother was a crack whore. She sexually abused him. Made him do things to her against his will. Disgusting, terrible things and sometimes she physically harmed him. Smashing empty liquor bottles over his head . . . putting out lit cigarettes against his skin . . . clawing his face with her ragged nails until he bled. Threatening she'd harm me if he didn't oblige. He hated her and grew to hate all women. Except for me. His little sister who took care of him. Whom he loved and protected. Adored and supported."

She paused, her eyes narrow and full of sorrow, and then they grew wild again, filling with fury. "It was my idea."

"To do what?" I asked feebly, shaking inside and instantly regretting my question.

"To obliterate her. To get rid of our sick piece of shit mother before she could inflict more damage. More pain."

I wasn't sure if I wanted to hear more of this twisted horror story, but my gut told me to hear her out.

"Drugging her was easy. She was drugged out to begin with. On a steady diet of heroin and booze. All we had to do was add a healthy dose of Xanax to her nightly nightcap when she wasn't looking. It was as easy as that. The two of us watched as she began to choke, then vomit, and finally lose consciousness. We took her pulse. Twice. She was still alive. The slightest moan lit a match under my brother. He wanted her to burn in hell for what she did to him and impulsively took her lighter and set her clothes on fire. Before the blaze spread to the rest of the house, we fled and watched as flames consumed the house, taking her with them. By the time the fire department and police arrived, the house was burned to the ground. And her body burned to the crisp. My innate acting skills coming in handy, I tearfully convinced the cops that our drunk, drug-addicted mother had likely conked out with a lit cigarette in her hand." An exaggerated sniff. "Poor mommy dearest!"

I was too in shock to stop her. How old were they when this all happened? To my surprise, she read my mind.

"Donny, as I affectionately called him, was eighteen. I was only twelve. We were free so we thought. He was; I wasn't. Not having any relatives—hell, we didn't even know who our father was or if he was one and the same—I was put into foster care while my brother left Vegas for Los Angeles to pursue his dream of getting into show business." Her eyes grew misty. "I'll never forget saying good-bye to him. It was the saddest day of my life. I was crying so hard I couldn't see straight and clinging to him. Blindly. Never wanting to let him go. He hugged me and told me, 'Lil sis, I'm gonna make it big and always take care of you.' And I promised to protect our secret."

"I kept my word; he kept his. He made it. And thanks to his lucrative career in television production, I was able to go to college, move to LA, and make a name for myself. My brother gave me everything! And you, *you* . . ."

Speechless, I watched as she yanked out the necklace she always wore hidden under her blouse. She dangled the pendant from between her fingers and I recognized it instantly. Springer's gaudy gold and diamond pinky ring! Then, she held it up, the boulder-size gem, glistening before me. Her eyes, two flaming embers, burned into mine.

"Thanks to you, this is all that remains of him. All I have left."

Despite the fear vibrating against my chest, I actually felt sorry for her. My voice softened. "I'm sorry."

She squeezed the ring in her fist so tightly her knuckles turned white. Her eyes grew wilder. "Sorry for what? Sorry for destroying his career? Sorry for taking away my only flesh and blood? Sorry for taking away the only person who ever cared about me?"

Her voice rose, growing more and more maniacal with every word. She was frightening me again. I needed to calm her down.

"Krystal, listen to me. A lot of people care about you. I do for one."

"SHUT. UP. BITCH. You don't know what it's like to be hurt so deeply you've lost a part of your life. I know what it feels like." She loosened her grip around the ring, letting it fall onto her clavicle. "And soon you will too. You're going to pay for what you did to my brother. My precious Donny!"

At her menacing words, fear surged inside me. In the distance, Scout's yelping grew louder. "Krystal, I need to let my dog out and you need to go."

"I'm not going anywhere until I have your confession on tape and the whole world knows what you did."

On impulse, I stepped in front of the lectern, not knowing my next move, and watched her reach into her briefcase. My vision caught sight of the gilded three-letter monogram: *KCS,* the bold font just like the one on Blake's overnight bag. Hoping he would magically appear, I was catapulted out of my wishful thinking by Krystal's shrill, piercing voice.

"Fuck your dog. You're not going anywhere either. Get back behind the lectern, you stupid bitch."

I froze in my tracks. Her eyes blazing with a mixture of fury and madness, she held me fiercely in her gaze.

And pointed a gun at my face.

"Let's get back to work."

Chapter 21
Blake

The morning swim felt good. After a frenetic week of all-day, back-to-back meetings both at the Bellagio, where I was staying, and the Vegas convention center, I felt refreshed. The NAB conference had gone well, and I'd learned a lot about the future of television. Everything was going digital and in no time, most people would be watching program content on their devices. The future for both big screen TVs and movie theaters was looking dismal. I made a note to tell my old man, the head of Conquest Broadcasting, to beef up emerging digital platforms R&D. To remain the leading global broadcaster, we needed to stay ten steps ahead. The future was now.

As I towel-dried myself, my cell phone rang. I picked it up from the small table next to my lounge chair. The blazing desert sun in my eyes, I squinted at the caller ID screen and recognized who was calling. It was Vera Nichols. My trustworthy and revered Vegas affiliate manager. I jabbed the green button and accepted the call.

"Hey Vera, what's up?"

"Blake, I'm afraid I have some bad news. I have to cancel lunch."

With Jen not coming to the conference with me, we had changed our dinner plans at her house to a barbecue lunch so I could get home sooner.

I sat down on the lounger. "What's going on?"

"It's Josh." Joshua was her precocious eight-year-old son, whom both Jen and I adored. I was even his godfather.

"What's wrong?" Concern underscored my voice.

"He woke up with a nasty bug and has been throwing up all morning."

I mentally let out a sigh of relief. Oh the joys of parenthood! So this is what I had to look forward to. I silently chortled, keeping the thought to myself as I'd not yet told Vera that Jen and I were having a baby.

"That's awful," I said.

Vera laughed. "You have no idea, especially what it feels like to be hit by projectile vomit."

"Yuck!"

"Yeah, totally yuck!" She chuckled. "I think it's best you don't come over. We don't want you to catch it."

"You know what they say, Vera. What happens in Vegas stays in Vegas."

"Yup, let's keep it that way." I could hear the smile

in her voice. "How 'bout a rain check when you come back? Next time with Jen."

"Deal." While I'd been looking forward to Steve's "famous" ribs and feigned disappointment, I was secretly thrilled with the turn of events. I mean, I wasn't happy Vera's kid was sick, but I was elated to be able to go home early to my tiger. Surprise her. Fuck her brains out as I'd not been able to have Skype-sex with her with my crazy busy schedule. Not even for five minutes.

Beneath my swim trunks, my cock high fived me. Mr. Burns was as excited as I was.

I missed my tiger terribly. I couldn't wait to see her.

And here's a little confession. Don't tell anyone.

I missed that damn dog too.

Chapter 22
Jennifer

The gun stayed pointed at me.

My chest was so tight I could barely breathe. Tears pricked the back of my eyes, but I willed them away. I needed to stay strong. Fierce. Not let the psychopath know I was terrified.

I clutched the lectern harder to maintain my balance. My head was spinning. *Think, Jen, think!*

Then blink. A light bulb went off.

"Krystal, if it's money you want, let me get my checkbook. I'll give you anything you want." My secret plan was to go to my bedroom and retrieve not only a check from my backpack, but also my secret weapon. My pepper spray, something I always carried with me . . . ever since her sicko brother almost raped me in college. I'd hand her the check and catching her off guard, spray her in the face with the blinding aerosol. Then escape as fast as I could.

Scout's incessant barking sounded in the distance. Another thought came to me. I could let him out of the bedroom with the hope he'd attack her. But on second thought, it was too risky. What if she shot him first? I shuddered at that possibility and quickly quashed it.

Mulling over my offer, the madwoman narrowed her eyes at me and sneered. "You fucking rich, entitled bitches. You think everything can go away by throwing money on the table. That's not going to work with me. I'm not after your worthless money."

So much for Plan A. I didn't have a Plan B. There was no reasoning with this crazed woman. My thudding heart was in my throat, my voice thick with fear.

"Krystal, what do you want?"

"It's simple. I want you to read the speech I've written and confess that you killed my brother. And don't leave out any bloody detail. Then, I'm going to upload it to YouTube for the whole world to view. By the time it goes viral, you won't be here."

Shaking, I processed her words. It boiled down to this: she was going to kill me! Bile rose to the back of my throat; my stomach twisted. I thought I might vomit.

"You're never going to get away with this!"

She scoffed at me. "You think I'm going to kill you?"

I swallowed hard past the golf ball-size lump in my throat. A cold shiver ran down the length of my spine. I couldn't get a word out if I tried.

"Let me answer that question for you, Jennifer. I'm

not going to kill you.'"

The tiniest sigh of relief spilled from my lungs. I inhaled and exhaled from my nose. Breathe in one . . . two . . . three. Breathe out one . . . two . . . three.

"What are you doing?" she snapped.

"Your breathing exercise. To calm myself."

She snorted. "So, you've actually learned something. Touché."

I'd also learned that perception was everything. I was going to play along with her sick game, whatever that was.

"Krystal, I'd like to read over the speech you prepared. So I don't screw it up." *And can buy myself some time,* I added silently.

"Fine." She fired the word at me. Better that than the gun. "I'll give you two minutes. That's it."

"Thank you," I murmured as she programmed the teleprompter. In the background, Scout was still barking madly and I could hear him scratching at the bedroom door.

"I wish you could shut up that awful beast," Krystal growled. "I don't know how you can concentrate. I should just put him down. Silence him forever."

"Please don't hurt him! He's just a puppy."

"Shut up, slut! Focus!"

My gaze returned to the teleprompter. As my eyes darted back and forth between the two screens, the shocking reality of what she was going to do to me hit me like a rockslide. Fast and hard. The terrifying bottom line: she *was* going to kill me! Except she was going to make it appear to be a suicide. I'd admit to destroying her brother, taking his life, and then stare straight into the camera and say I could no longer live with my all-consuming guilt. I'd do a final tearful apology before the screen went black.

Then bang! A bullet to my head. Fired by Krystal!

"Time's up," I heard her say and caught her glancing down at her gold watch. The gun was still in her hand, aimed at me. I could already hear the blast in my head and then out of the blue, the words of Blake's shrewd father whirled in my head. Ones he attributed to making him to one of the most powerful and successful businessmen in the world.

You gotta fight fire with fire.

I had no choice. Maybe it was going to work, maybe it wasn't. I was going to fight crazy with crazy.

"I'm ready," I said in my strongest voice. *Ready or not, here I come.* My beloved father's voice echoed in my head. The words he always said when we played hide-and-seek. I was playing a whole new game. *Go for It!*

Uncrossing her ankles, Krystal began to tap one of her stilettos on the hardwood floor. *Tap, tap, tap, tap.* Drowning out the sound of Scout's barking. *Woof, woof, woof, woof.* And my thudding heart. *Thump, thump, thump, thump.*

My eyes met hers. "I'm going to start from the top, if that's okay with you."

She grinned wickedly, her evil smile reminiscent of her brother's. "An excellent idea. It'll make the speech way more coherent and easier to edit."

Fortifying myself with another lungful of air, I began, repeating back the first two lines of the speech she'd written.

Then . . .

"I'm standing here before Krystal Clare Springer, a mentally disturbed woman, who is pointing a gun at me with the intention of shooting me. She is blaming me for the death of her brother, Don Springer, a sick evil man who sexually assaulted me. On more than one occasion. I did *not k*ill him! He tried to kill me! If you don't believe me, contact the Los Angeles Police Department. It's all on file. You must believe—"

She cut me off. Sharp, fast, and furious. Her cheeks burning crimson, she parroted my earlier words.

"That's *not* what I wrote!"

My eyes shot up and then they grew wide. One of my hands flew to my mouth.

My heart skipped a beat.

Oh my God! I couldn't believe it.

Chapter 23
Blake

Jesus. What clusterfuck had I just walked into? What the hell was my wife saying? And why?

I stopped dead in my tracks and about twenty feet away, my gaze met Jen's. A mixture of terror and surprise flickered in her eyes; her jaw hung open, and she was white as a ghost.

Still holding my leather overnight bag, I took in my surroundings. The lectern with my frightened wife standing behind it... the video equipment... the teleprompter... and a woman with an auburn bob who was seated in an armchair, her back to me. In the background, I could hear Scout barking madly and scratching at something. He must be locked up in our bedroom.

"Jen, what's going on?" I tried to keep my voice steady. Keep my cool.

Before she could utter a word, the mysterious woman jerked her head and glared at me. Venom poured from her eyes.

"What the fuck are *you* doing here?"

I live here, lady. Who the fuck are you? That's what I wanted to say, but Jen stopped me.

"Blake, she's Don Springer's sister and she has a gun!"

As Jen's words sunk in, the woman sprung to her feet. Facing me. The gun in her hand, pointed at me. "And, you're Blake. The slut's husband."

I didn't acknowledge her. My pulse in overdrive, I instead replayed fragments of Jen's speech I'd just heard in my head. *A mentally disturbed woman . . . she is blaming me for the death of her brother.*

Not moving a muscle, I stared at her straight in the eye. "Krystal, you've got it wrong. My wife didn't kill your brother." A pregnant pause. "I did! It's me you want!"

"No, Blake!" Jen screamed out as Krystal pondered my words. She gave my tiger a sideways glance and then, with a sneer, refocused on me. A witch-like cackle accompanied her wicked smile.

"Maybe I should just shoot you both."

"You won't get away with this! Walk away, and we'll pretend this never happened." I was lying through my teeth. I was going to put this woman away. I swear over my dead body.

She snorted. "Seriously, Blake, do you think I'm that stupid? I honestly pegged you for being a lot smarter than you are. You stupid fuck!"

"We'll even give you a million dollars in cash. Anything you want!" Panic began to fill my voice.

With a look of contempt, she rolled her eyes. "You're just like your pathetic whore wife. Thinking money is the answer to all your problems." She paused, and her voice grew louder and angrier by decibels. "All the money in the world can't bring back my brother, you fuckshit!"

My heart hammered; my mind raced. She was smart. She was determined. She was irrational. A bona fide psycho bitch.

As I frantically pondered a new tactic, she brandished the gun in Jen's direction, then mine. "Eenie, meenie, minie, moe. Hmm . . . who should go first?" Lifting her free hand, she pressed her thumb under her chin and tapped her zip-locked lips with her index finger. She was either stalling or thinking. Time was running out. I had to make a move. Come up with something.

Still dangling from my hand, the weight of my heavy overnight bag was making my arm ache. A momentary distraction, but suddenly—bing!—an idea came to me. It was worth a shot. Even if it meant dislocating my shoulder. With a fortifying breath, I lifted up the bag, and with a grunt and all the muscle power I had, flung it twenty feet across the room at the pyscho.

"Huh!" groaned the stunned Krystal as it struck her

in the chest, knocking her to the floor. And the gun out of her hand. I couldn't believe my luck! I should have been an Olympic discus thrower.

"Run, Jen!" I screamed out as the disoriented woman crouched on the floor. Dazed and confused, clutching her chest. The gun by her side, a hand's reach away.

My heart pounding against my chest like a jackhammer, my eyes stayed fixed on my tiger as she leaped from behind the lectern and took off like the wind. Thank goodness, she'd taken up running since being with me.

"Run, baby, run!" I shouted as I ran to meet her halfway. In my peripheral vision, I could see Krystal scrambling to get up, the gun back in her hand. "Hurry!"

Then before I could blink, the unexpected happened.

"Jen!" I cried out as I watched her trip with a gasp and go flying across the floor. My Calamity Jen! Her goddamn heel had gotten caught in one of the teleprompter's cable wires.

I dashed to her side. She was sprawled out on her stomach, her hands anchored by her shoulders as if she was trying to push herself up.

"Jen, Jen, are you all right?"

No response. Panic surged. My heart clenched in my chest.

"Talk to me, tiger. Please talk to me!" *Let me hear you roar.*

"Yes," she finally breathed out as she staggered to her feet with my help. And then she winced, her right leg buckling.

"What's wrong?"

"Blake, I think I twisted my ank—"

Not letting her finish her sentence, I scooped her up into my arms. "C'mon. Let's get the hell out of here."

"You're not going anywhere." The familiar razor-sharp voice. "This is the end of the road for you two murderous scumbags."

Carrying Jen, I spun around. Staggering toward us, her perfectly coiffed hair in disarray, her prim suit covered in dust, the psycho bitch smirked, her assassinous eyes shooting daggers. Glinting with wicked determination.

The gun in her hand aimed at both of us.

Chapter 24
Jennifer

Blake's heart was pounding as fast and loudly as mine. I could feel it in my bones, hear it in my ears. An overwhelming feeling of sadness, fear, and hopelessness washed over me, and perhaps it could all be summed up in one word. Despair.

Our short life together was coming to an end. A horrible, tragic end. I was going to lose my beloved husband. And him, me. We were both going to die at the hands of this sick, ruthless woman. We'd never see our dear friends or family again. Or our dog. And this: we'd never meet our precious baby!

Tears pricked my eyes. Why did Don Springer have to come into my life? Follow me from college to Conquest. I thought he was finally out of it after Blake beat the life out of him, but he never left. He was always there, hiding in the spirit of his sinister sibling, as loyal as she was screwed up. A hot tear escaped one eye and trickled down my cheek.

"Stop crying, you little bitch!" Still pointing the gun

at us, now held firmly in both hands, Krystal scrunched up her face. "You don't know what it's like to lose someone you love."

"I do!!" I wanted to shout back, but as the searing tears kept coming, I could only tell Blake how much I loved him in the softest of voices. A mere whisper.

"Tiger, I love you too," he rasped back as our soon-to-be killer curled her right index finger around the trigger. It was all too much. I broke into heaving sobs and clung to Blake's neck like a vise, my head resting against his rock hard chest. Like a "Best of" retrospective show, all the wonderful memories of our time together played randomly in my head in no chronological order. Beginning with that very first time I kissed him blindfolded and knew my life was changed forever ... Our surprise Christmas in July wedding ... Our first slow dance in Vegas ... My first Shabbat at his parents' house when I accidentally saw his manhood for the first time ... Our walk with Scout and the Shitstick ... That time we broke a motel bed while fucking our brains out ... The snow angels ... All those thoughtful, unexpected gifts ... That first Christmas kiss under the mistletoe ... And every kiss ever since.

Oh, those delicious, kissable lips! I so needed his lips on mine. One last time. With rivers of tears, I lifted my head and looked up at him. As if he'd been reading my mind or thinking the same things, his lips curled into the smallest of smiles, just enough to make those dimples shine, and then his head angled down, and on my next strangled breath, his lips touched down on mine. So warm and soft like a blanket of love. I let my mouth succumb to his, parting my lips so his velvety tongue could enter and do its final dance. Our last tango.

I wanted it to last forever. I wanted us to last forever. *Until death do us part.* My heart throbbed, my body ached. That vow wasn't meant to be. Fate had betrayed us. Hot tears in my throat, my lips trembled against Blake's in a mad frenzy of passion and lust.

"That's it!" hissed Krystal. Finality in her brash, booming voice. We were one click away from doom.

But that didn't stop us. Blake deepened the kiss, sucking on my lips as my hands cupped his stubbled jaw, drawing him closer to me. If we were going to die, this is how it would be. Just like the lovers in *The Kiss* painting Blake had given me. *Oneness.* And if we were lucky, one bullet would be fired at close range. Going through my body straight through his. Piercing my heart. His heart. We'd die in unison, sparing each of us the unbearable anguish of seeing the other die first. Letting us fall together in a crumpled heap. Our inseparable limbs entangled. Twisted into a lovers' infinity knot.

I wanted to stay lost in the moment. Never let go of my beloved, beautiful husband. The man who loved me. Protected me. And was my superhero. *That Man.*

Yet, every man, no matter how strong and powerful, or as invincible as he seemed, had his kryptonite. Something that could rob him of his superpowers. Make him vulnerable. Blake had his.

A loaded gun.

Click.

Then, a thunderous bang.

And a flash of black.

Chapter 25
Blake

"Oh my God! Get this fucking beast off me!" shrieked Krystal, flailing her arms as she tried to free herself from our dog Scout, who was barking and growling like there was no tomorrow. Which up until this minute was a grim reality.

It all happened so fast. The attack. Scout had managed to break out of our bedroom, knocking down the door with a thunderous crash. Startling Jen and me out of our kiss, he'd flown into the living room like a scud missile—a black blip—and made a beeline for our assailant, catching her off guard.

"Don't just stand there!" she cried out again as our relentless Scout shredded her suit with his teeth, standing on his hind legs with his big paws on her shoulders. "Help me!"

"Blake, what should we do?" Though she was right next to me, my frightened Jen had to shout above the deafening cacophony of Krystal's frantic shrieks and our dog's rabid barks.

Still holding her in my arms, I didn't answer. The problem was that the crazy bitch was still gripping the loaded gun in one hand. She was a loose cannon. Dangerous and unpredictable. I weighed my options and the outcomes. Yes, I could try to pull Scout off her or kick the gun out of her hand, but who knew if she'd use it first. Kill me. My wife. Our dog. One or all three of us.

Scratch that.

I could also try to get Jen and myself to safety. Out of the living room or even better the apartment. But there was no easy escape route as we'd have to skirt by the gun-wielding maniac any which way we fled. Our chances were fifty-fifty at best.

Scratch that.

Finally, I could try calling 911. But that was impossible because my phone was in my jacket, which I'd left in the entryway and Jen's was who the hell knows where. She was always losing or misplacing it.

Scratch that.

That left only one choice. To let Scout go at the psycho bitch. Tear her to pieces. Turn her into dog meat.

Go, boy, go!

Jennifer

I clung to Blake as I watched Scout maul Krystal, the hairs on his backside bristling like a porcupine and his head jerking left and right, up and down as he tore off her clothing. A vicious tug of war that Scout was winning. My heart pounding against my rib cage, I silently cheered him on.

Krystal's clothes were in tatters. Our unstoppable dog had even torn off the sleeve of her jacket. Standing on his hind legs, he was in her face, his jaw snapping at her madly, slobber pouring from his mouth.

"Get this fucking monster off me!" she screamed again, terror written all over her contorted face.

Her hysterics only aggravated Scout, making him more aggressive. More relentless. More vicious.

"Scout!" I called out at the top of my lungs, but he ignored me and began tearing at the collar of her red silk blouse, determined to rip it off. With a hiss, one side of it detached, exposing the necklace with Don Springer's diamond pinky ring.

"GRRRR!" growled Scout louder as he played tug of war with the thick chain, trying to yank it off her neck, shaking his head back and forth vehemently. It was only then I realized it was the very same obnoxious gold chain that Don Springer wore around his neck.

"Stop him!" screeched Krystal, her arms flailing

and her voice hoarse.

The fear vibrating in my chest gave way to a spark of hope. My breath hitched in my throat. Scout was winning. He had the upper hand and was going to take her down. Then, suddenly, without warning, victory was cut short by a violent thrust as Scout's prey whacked him on his skull with the metal gun. My fur baby yelped in pain, then she hit him again and again. Pistol-whipping him!

"Blake," I sobbed, "she's going to kill him!" I watched in horror, my heart beating in my throat, as Scout withstood each bone-shattering blow, growing weaker and weaker with each successive one. His yelps morphed into whimpers. Then, moans as he sagged to the floor in a crumpled heap. His front paws protectively curled on top of his bleeding head. His body limp. Unable to stand up.

Scalding hot tears rushed down my face. My poor baby boy! My fur baby! I had to save him. Just as he'd tried to save me. My brave, loyal, loving dog! I owed him my life! And I owed him his!

With a bolt of adrenaline that obliterated the shooting pain in my ankle, I jumped out of Blake's arms.

"Jesus, Jen!" he cried out. "What are you doing?"

I was going to save our dog!

He risked his life! I was going to risk mine.

Then, *BANG!*

Blake

What the hell was my wife doing?

Plain and simple. And crazy as shit. She was limping into the battlefield, like a delirious, wounded soldier armed with fierce determination. And out for revenge. My heart jumped as another gunshot whisked by her and ricocheted off the back wall.

"Jen, get down!"

"Fuck her! Fuck you!" screamed Krystal, her face purple with rage, her eyes wild with madness. She recklessly fired again and as she did, I lunged at my tiger, knocking her flat to the floor. My supine body sheathing her like protective armor, I could feel her labored breathing beneath my weight. Thank God, she was still alive.

"Blake," I heard her mumble. "Scout!"

"Shh!" I whispered in her ear. "Don't move."

I felt her acknowledge me with the tiniest of nods. Slowly, I raised my head just a few inches and gazing up, met Krystal's deranged eyes. Smirking, she pointed the gun at me.

"You've made it so easy for me, Blake Fucking Burns. First you. Then your slut for a wife. So much for you being her white knight in shining armor."

"Krystal, I'm sorry I killed your brother. It was an accident. I didn't mean to."

Her brows lifted to her razor-sharp bangs. "An accident? You honestly want me to believe that?"

"It's the truth." And the quasi-truth it was as the memory of that fatal night played in my head. No, I couldn't stop stabbing Springer with the tip of Jen's crutch or whacking him with it. I was like a pilot on autodrive. "I got carried away!"

"Shut up! One more word and I'll blow a bullet through your ugly skull before I count to three."

One more word.

In my tiger's self-defense course, she'd learned to yell "fire" to get someone's attention or distract an assailant. That word of all words wasn't going to work here. If I uttered it, she'd shoot me. Fire the gun.

A horrifying mixture of despair and desperation swept over me. I'd run out of magical thinking. Our lives were over. I was about to tell my tiger how much I love her one last time when I heard a rumble and felt the building shake. Every muscle in my body quivered like I was having an orgasm. But this was no orgasm. Holy shit. We were having an earthquake! A big one! In the kitchen, I could hear plates rattling and nearby on the bar, several wineglasses shattered. Then, with a crash, Krystal's tripod with the video camera toppled over.

"Oh my God!" shrieked Krystal, terror in her voice,

as the apartment kept shaking. Her face blanched, her body teetered, and the gun shook in her trembling hands.

Yet another tremor and I sprung to my feet, ready to lunge at her.

And at the very same time, to my wide-eyed shock, so did Scout, jumping onto his hind legs as if he was wearing springs on his back paws. He was alive!

Not stopping, I heard Krystal scream. Part in shock. Part in pain. Growling ferociously, Scout was all over her, blood spouting from her neck.

A blast of gunfire.

BAM! And then all turned to black.

Chapter 26
Jennifer

Silence.

The calm after the storm.

But this had been a storm like none other. A major earthquake, the likes of which I'd never experienced. And an explosive gunshot fired in the height of it.

I was afraid to open my eyes.

Afraid of what I might see.

Pure, unadulterated fear consumed me.

My body was still trembling and my breathing was labored. Still stretched out face down on the floor, every muscle in my body ached. I blinked my eyes several times, squeezing out tears like one of those Squeegee mops my mom loved.

Slowly, hesitantly, bravely, I lifted myself up, first into a cobra position and then onto all fours. Prying my eyes open, part in silent prayer, part in heart-pounding fear, I took in my surroundings and my jaw fell to the floor.

Oh my God! The place was a disaster. But I didn't

give a damn about the broken glasses or ceramic planters. Or the priceless chandelier, a gift from Blake's mother, that had fallen and shattered on our dining table.

I gasped and a hand flew to my mouth.

Before me was carnage. A pile up of three bodies surrounded by a pool of blood. Krystal's face up, all the color drained from her, and Scout and Blake facedown, sprawled on top of her. Neither of them moved.

As if we were having another earthquake, a violent tremor shot through me. I felt the earth open beneath me, then swallow me whole. *NO!* I silently screamed. *Please God, NO!*

I'd lost my husband! I'd lost our dog!

Grief latched onto me like a suction cup, sucking all the air out of my lungs. My chest tightened so much I thought I was suffocating. Bile rose to the back of my throat and as I was about to throw up, my watering eyes grew wide. Could it be?

Blake was moving his fingers. He was alive!

"Blake!" I breathed out, springing to my feet and ignoring the pain that shot up my right ankle. Slowly, he stood up and I hobbled toward him as fast as I could. We met each other halfway and held each other in a vise-like embrace. The tears I'd held back sprung to my eyes and fell freely down my cheeks.

"Oh Blake, I thought I'd lost you. That she shot you. That you were d—"

He silenced me with a tender kiss, then gently cupped my face with his hands, his beautiful blue eyes burning into mine. "Shh! You know I'd never leave you. I'm *That Man*, remember? Your superhero."

Blinking back tears, I nodded. He was my superhero. My husband. My lover. My soul mate. My protector. The soon-to-be father of our baby. My everything. Then, I glanced down and gasped again. There was a huge bright red patch on the side of his shirt. Blood! "Oh my God, Blake. She did hurt you! You're bleeding!" There was also blood all over my hand from where I'd touched him.

Blake lowered his eyes. "Baby, I'm fine." He gave me a reassuring smile and then his face darkened. "Jesus!"

My gaze immediately shot across the room. My panic button went off. Scout was still sprawled on top of an unconscious Krystal, the crimson pool around them expanding rapidly. He wasn't moving. Not a muscle! A horrific, bone-chilling shudder of reality came over me.

"Oh my God, Blake! It's Scout! She killed him!"

"Tiger, stay here!" Apprehension etched deep on his face, he sprinted over to our motionless dog. There was no way I was staying behind. I loved this dog from here to the moon and back. He was my fur baby. My precious fur baby. Wincing with every step, I followed Blake, tears in my eyes, my two-ton heart in my throat.

My poor, sweet Scout! When I caught up to Blake, he was on his knees next to Scout, one hand on his back. The sight of my lifeless dog was all too much for me. I broke into uncontrollable sobs.

"Jen, Jen! He's alive. He's still breathing!" My husband gazed up at me. "Feel!"

Wordlessly, I brushed away my tears. Crouching down next to Blake, I let him take my tear-stained hand and place it on Scout's silky back. I let out a gasp. Or was it a sigh of relief? Beneath my palm, I could feel the rise and fall of Scout's chest. It was ever so slight, but it was real. Scout was alive! My skin tingled with hope, but it was fleeting. The puddle of blood around us had gotten bigger! Fear poured back into my veins. My stomach clenched.

"Blake! He's still bleeding! We need to do something!"

"Quick! Call Dr. Chase. Where's your phone?"

"In the bedroom. On the nightstand."

"I'll get it. Stay here with Scout. I'm going to get my phone, too, and call 911."

"Okay." My voice was a tearful rasp.

As Blake dashed off, I curled into a sitting position on the floor, putting my cheek against Scout and stroking him gently with my hand. I wept quietly, my hot tears soaking his coat.

"Please don't die, baby boy! I love you so much! Promise me you won't."

Softly, I began to sing to him. Our song. The special one that belonged to Blake and me. "The First Time Ever I Saw Your Face."

As the words slowly spilled from my quivering lips, that first time I saw Scout at the West LA Shelter rushed into my head. His big brown expressive eyes! His smiling mouth! That look on his face that said take me home with you! Yes, the first time ever I saw his face I knew he was meant to be mine.

I don't know if he could hear me singing, but I continued anyway, each word more choked than the one before. I could barely get out another one because tears were clogging my throat. Then, suddenly, he let out a little moan and moved his tail a millimeter. My heart flooded with emotion. He heard me! My fur baby heard me!

And so did Blake. He was back, crouching down beside me. "He heard me! Scout heard me!"

A small, sad smile twitched on his lips. The sadness in his smile zapped my snippet of optimism. He handed me my phone; his was in his jeans pocket.

"I already called 911. What's Dr. Chase's number?"

"I have it on speed-dial." Thank goodness, I'd added his name to my list of contacts. I quickly found it and hit call.

The phone rang five times. It felt like an eternity. My heart hammering, I feared the call would go to his voicemail or an answering service. It was Sunday and his office was likely closed. Then, finally on the next ring, he picked up. Thank God!

"Jen, hi! What can I do—?"

I cut him off. My voice panicked, tearful. "Dr. Chase, Scout's been shot."

"Jesus. Where?"

"I think in his abdomen."

No further questions asked. His tone remained calm and collected. "Hold a tight compress to the wound. Text me your address. I'm going to call Pet Medevac to transport him to the VCA. They have the best team of canine surgeons in the state. I'll meet you there."

Five minutes later, sirens were blaring in our ears. Red lights flashing in the driveway twenty stories below.

And the white towel we were holding against Scout's bullet hole was now soaked.

Crimson red.

Chapter 27
Blake

Scout wasn't the only one critically wounded in the life and death showdown.

When Jen and I maneuvered him so we could put a compress to his wound, we discovered that he'd bit Krystal in the neck. Like Scout, she was hemorrhaging, the blood spurting like a fountain. He must have hit an artery. There was blood everywhere, her white suit soaked red. I thought Jen might faint, but my brave tiger surprised me and didn't. While she held the compress, I took Krystal's pulse.

"Is she still alive?" Jen asked anxiously.

Springer's sister had a faint pulse, but I wanted to say no. Pretend she was dead and let the fucking bitch, who almost killed us all, bleed out. But then the scrawny, unconscious woman let out a faint moan and gave it away that she was still alive.

"Blake, we need to do something! We can't let her die!"

I just didn't get my wife sometimes. Screw Krystal.

This sick piece of shit woman deserved to die. She was a murderer. Just like her sorry ass brother. They deserved to rot in hell together.

She moaned again, turning her head slightly. Jen moved closer to me. "Blake, I'll stay here and hold Scout's compress. Make another one for Krystal. We've got to control the bleeding."

Reluctantly, I did as she asked. A few minutes later, we were like a first responder team, with me holding a compress to Scout's abdomen, Jen to the psycho's neck with both hands. I secretly wished it was the other way around. I'd just dab her neck and let her bleed. Or press too hard and cut off her air supply.

The police followed by the paramedics arrived, the latter relieving me of my duty. They couldn't take her out on the gurney fast enough. Good-bye and good riddance! I let one of the kind EMTs help me attend to Scout while we waited for the pet transport; another treated Jen's ankle, wrapping it in an Ace bandage. It was thankfully just a mild sprain and with RICE—rest, ice, compression, and elevation—it would heal soon.

The PetVac team arrived shortly afterward. By then, our apartment was in a state of chaos. In addition to the mess from the earthquake, it was swarmed by an army of uniformed cops, plain-clothes detectives, crime scene investigators, and forensic specialists. Our entire living room had been cordoned off with wide yellow tape and looked like a scene straight out of our popular Conquest crime series, *Criminal Justice*. For both Jen and me, it was déjà-vu, reminding us of the night I stopped Don Springer from killing her. How could this happen to us twice? What were the odds? One in a gazillion? Then, I remembered my father's rule of statistics: things either happen or they don't. So one in two. Fifty-fifty.

I kept an arm around Jen's shoulders as the PetVac team carefully lifted our limp, unconscious Scout onto a gurney. They had managed to stop the bleeding by binding his middle, and numerous IVs were attached to him. Even my heart sunk at the sight of him. Jen sniffled.

"Blake, I want to go with him!"

I did too. But unfortunately, we couldn't. The CSI unit needed us to stay put. They wanted to interrogate us. It was going to be a long, agonizing day.

~~~

We finally got to the VCA hospital in the mid afternoon. Three forty-five to be exact. Holding Jen's hand, we raced up to the check-in. That buxom redhead, who we'd encountered the first time we were here, was sitting behind the console behind her computer. Frizzball.

"We're here for our dog Scout," Jen said breathlessly. "He's in surgery."

The attendant's eyes lifted and glinted with recognition. "I remember you two! And now you're all over the Internet."

I bristled. We were already headline news. In this digital age of social media, news traveled fast. I bet Conquest Broadcasting would be running the story on its five o'clock local news broadcast with Skye Collins. It could even be the lead story since Conquest favored ratings-getting sensational news. Dammit. My parents would find out about our life and death experience online or on TV before hearing it from me. They were on their way to Australia and I hadn't been able to reach them.

"How's Scout doing?" asked Jen, her voice jittery and filled with trepidation.

"Let me call back to the operating room." I gripped my tiger's hand harder as the woman picked up a desk phone and dialed an extension. My eyes stayed glued on her jowly face, looking for any sign. Good or bad. She simply nodded and hung up the phone.

"He's still in surgery."

Shit. He'd been here for hours. "When will he be out?"

She shrugged. "I have no idea. Why don't the two of you have a seat? Someone will let me know."

I let out an exasperated breath. For the second time, I wanted to punch her. Until her expression softened and she said, "We're all rooting for him."

Jen and I sat side by side in the crowded waiting room. Silently. My cell phone muted. Now dressed in comfy sweats instead of that hideous pantsuit which I planned to burn, she held my hand while her other iced her ankle, the ice pack courtesy of the animal hospital.

Thirty anxious minutes later, my tiger excused herself to use the restroom.

Shortly after she disappeared, a plainly dressed silver-haired woman wearing a large cross around her neck took the other vacant chair next to me. Lying on the floor by her side was a large, handsome Golden Retriever. She turned to me, her face kind and reassuring.

"He's going to be okay. Your dog is brave and strong. What a wonderful animal!"

She, too, must have seen the story on the Internet. I wanted to believe her. Her crinkly eyes exuded warmth and compassion. While I was in no mood for conversation, I asked her why she was here. Her Retriever looked perfectly healthy.

"Nemo had an in-grown toenail. This is a follow-up visit. We drove down here from Santa Barbara."

"Wow! That's far away. What made you come all the way here?"

She smiled. "We love this hospital. Especially Dr.

Chase who used to work here. He's treated all our therapy dogs."

"Therapy dogs?"

"Yes. I work at a rehabilitation facility. We use trained therapy dogs to work with our patients. They can make such a big difference in a person's life and help them heal faster, both mentally and physically." She glanced down at her big copper-colored dog. "Nemo is one of our best. Both our patients and staff love him."

"He's a beautiful dog." He truly was with his lustrous coat and expressive face.

"Thank you. All dogs are beautiful."

I reflected on her words. The truth is, I'd never really seen an ugly dog. Some were funny looking, but I wouldn't go as far as calling them ugly.

"Do you know that dog is God spelled backwards?"

D-O-G. G-O-D. She was right! Strangely, I'd never made that connection.

"There is God in every dog. I believe they are heaven-sent."

"Do you mean like angels?"

"Yes. They are guardian angels. They are here on earth to love and protect us."

Her words went straight to my heart. And I thought about Scout. He'd saved our lives! Even taken a bullet for me. He *was* our guardian angel. I felt overwhelmed with emotion. Scout couldn't die! It just wasn't fair.

Frizzball's booming voice broke into my distraught thoughts. "Sister Marie . . . Nemo. Dr. Rattan is ready for you."

"That's us!" beamed the woman next to me, who was obviously a nun. "Come on, Nemo." The big dog sprung to his feet and began to pant excitedly.

Sister Marie collected her minimal belongings and then she placed one of her large hands on top of mine. It was warm and comforting. She held me in her soulful gaze.

"Tell your lovely wife I'm going to pray for your dog. God bless you all."

She rose and I thanked her. She was a special human being. Fate had put her in my life. As she strode off with Nemo, a newfound spirituality washed over me. An unexpected, profound lightness of being.

Pray. That's all we could do.

I wasn't very religious, but believed in the power of prayer. When Jen had her hysterectomy and was facing a possible diagnosis of cancer, that's what I did. And it worked.

It could work again. Hope filled me.

C'mon, Scout. You've got this. You make it home and I'll even let you have one of Jen's G-strings.

―――

The minutes ticked like hours. It was close to five

o'clock and the sun-filled sky had begun to darken. My stomach growled. Except for the Starbucks coffee and muffin I'd grabbed at Vegas's McCarran airport, I hadn't eaten all day, but I wasn't hungry. The only thing I craved was news of our Scout. Good news!

I was about to nod off when a familiar raspy voice, calling out our names, startled me. Jen, who'd fallen asleep against me, startled, too, and bolted to an upright position.

Dr. Chase!

Heading toward us, he was wearing scrubs and looked exhausted. A five o'clock shadow laced his jaw. Both Jen and I jumped to our feet. My heart beating a mile a minute, I squeezed Jen's hand.

"How is he, doc?" The words flew out of my mouth.

"He's one hell of a dog."

"He's okay?" stammered Jen.

"Yup, he's going to be okay."

"Oh my God! Thank goodness!" Tears filled Jen's eyes and she flung her arms around Dr. Chase. Under any other circumstances, jealousy would have flooded me and I might have punched him in the gut. But right now, all I wanted to do was hug him too. Don't tell anyone!

Relief washed over us as Dr. Chase filled us in. Our superdog had sailed through the five-hour operation. They'd opened him up and retrieved the bullet. It took thirty-five sutures to close him up, something that made us both shudder. But Dr. Chase reassured us that there was nothing to worry about. They'd also sewn up the gash on his head with another nine stitches. Fortunately, an MRI showed there was no brain damage.

"Can we take him home?" Jen asked anxiously.

Dr. Chase shook his head. "We want to keep him here a few days for observation. Make sure he doesn't get an infection and can eat properly."

He went on to tell us that Scout was going to have to get used to his new outfit—a girdle-like bandage around his middle and a cone around his head to prevent him from tearing at the dressing. He was also going to have to be on a soft diet for several weeks until his stomach lining healed.

"Like matzo balls and noodle kugel?" I bet Grandma, who adored Scout, was going to have a field day.

Dr. Chase laughed. "Yeah, that would work. Bring me some too!"

Jen and I shared the laugh as our vet reached into a pocket.

"Oh, I almost forgot. We found something else in his stomach."

My brows lifted in wonderment as he withdrew his hand, his fingers fisted. Slowly, he uncurled them.

Jen's emerald eyes lit up like lanterns. "Oh my God! Don Springer's pinky ring!"

Holy shit! I couldn't believe it. The gaudy diamond

ring shone in my eyes. Our dog must have swallowed it when he took a chunk out of Krystal's neck. Dessert!

Dr. Chase lightly touched the platinum and diamond unicorn broach that was pinned to my tiger's hoodie. Jen had insisted on wearing it because she truly believed it brought us good luck. She was right.

The vet chuckled. "I thought Scout had better taste in jewelry."

"Me too!" Taking the ring from him and shoving it into a pocket, I couldn't help but laugh as well. Operation Chasehole had bit the dust. Okay, he was a handsome rake, had a little bit of a thing for my wife, but I actually liked Chase Sexton. He was smart, funny, and caring. Best of all, he'd helped save our dog's life. I had a feeling we were going to be buds.

"So, doc, can we see our dog before we take off?"

"Absolutely. He's in recovery, but he may be up by now. Follow me."

~~~

The recovery room was a smallish room on the second floor of the building. There was an attendant and several beds, but Scout was the only animal occupying one. He was lying on a soft blanket and appeared to be asleep.

My tiger stopped dead in her tracks upon seeing him and gasped. Even I wasn't prepared to see him hooked up to so many monitors and IVs. I hated anything that resembled a needle. My stomach churned. Plus, his head was shaved where they'd given him stitches. Dr. Chase had assured us that his hair would grow back over time and that in a few months we would not even be able to see a scar. The same with the incision along his underside. But still.

"Oh my God, Blake. Our poor baby! His bandage is so big!"

It was pretty massive. A mishmash of gauze, elastic, and adhesive tape that wrapped around almost his entire torso. He wasn't yet wearing the cone of shame, as my father used to call those things. Though for our heroic Scout, it was more like a crown of honor. Scout's honor.

Holding hands, our fingers threaded, we inched closer to him. Each step, a little less hesitant. Up close, we could see his breathing was even and he wasn't manifesting any signs of agitation.

"Baby, do you think he's in pain?" Jen asked.

"Nah. Dr. Chase said they shot him up with some painkillers and he's also on them intravenously."

Standing by his side, Jen bent over and gave him a tender kiss on his head, careful not to go near his stitches. I petted him gently. My heart swelled with emotion. I never thought I'd be so happy to see the dog I didn't want. I owed him my life.

Suddenly, he lifted his head a little and his eyes slid

open. They were glazed from the anesthesia, but glinted with recognition.

"Scout!" Jen's voice rose, growing brighter. "Mommy and Daddy are here! We love you so much!"

Scout raised his head a little more and that goofy tongue-driven smile of his or whatever it was lit up his face. Even his tail wagged! And then as fast as his eyes opened, they shut again though the content smile on his face remained.

His light snoring was like music to my ears. I took Jen into my arms and engulfed her in my warmth. And my love. I pressed my lips on her head, and we both wept. All the tension of the day melted away. Replaced by tears of gratitude. Tears of joy.

We held each other. Did a slow dance. Our hearts and bodies melded.

Without warning, as I swayed my wife, a stench filled the room. A too familiar scent. A deadly but silent stink bomb.

I silently laughed. Squeezed my tiger tighter.

That dog was back!

And he was here to stay.

Chapter 28

Blake

One Year Later

"*Happy Birthday to you! Happy Birthday to you!*"

The fluffy duvet pulled down below my knees, I felt a warm naked body straddling mine, soft, silky lips fluttering across my chest, shoulders, and neck.

Groggily with a contented moan, I peeled one eye open, then the other. My tiger! Thank fuck, it wasn't Scout!

Stark naked, her hair loose, she clutched my shoulders, teased my lips, and began rocking her body against mine as she continued to sing to me. My morning wood already buried deep inside her, her lovely breasts grazing my chest. Man, I loved this. My tiger was doing all the work. All I had to do was lay back and meet her slow, sensual, rhythmic bucks. Enjoy the ride. It felt fan-fucking-tastic. Birthday fucks were the best.

"Mmm," I murmured. "And Happy Anniversary."

December 21st. My thirty-second birthday. And our second anniversary.

The bedroom door was shut. But as we got close to reaching our climaxes, our breaths growing ragged, there was a scratching at the door. And a wail from the nursery next door.

Jen picked up her pace.

And I came. We both did. Hard.

Still clinging to my shoulders, Jen lifted her head and her glazed *après le fuck* eyes latched onto mine. A wry smile curled up her lips.

"This is the first of your many birthday surprises."

"Really?"

I had a few surprises in store for her too. Later tonight, after I fucked her brains out, I was going to present her with the gorgeous onyx pin I had custom-made by my mother's jeweler. And hidden deep in my sock drawer, far away from the likes of Scout. Believe me, I never wanted a repeat of the unicorn incident. This pin was a replica of our dog, complete with a ruby-studded red collar and a pair of chocolate diamond eyes. On the back, I'd inscribed the date and *Woof! I love you!*

Yup. No bones about it. I fucking loved my wife. More than ever if more was possible.

It was a monumental day. Not only my birthday and our second anniversary. It was also almost the five-month birthday of our son Leo, who was born on July 23rd. And the fourteen-month anniversary of when we'd conceived him in a petri dish and had his embryo transferred into my sister Marcy's uterus. As I devoured the delicious, maple syrup-soaked pancakes and bacon my tiger had made, happiness filled every molecule of my being. Our lives had changed so much over the last two years. Especially the past one.

We had a dog. We had a baby. We had a new house. I reflected on all these things as I watched Jen spoon-feed cereal to our son Leo, clad in his too-cute-for-words SpongeBob pajamas. "Open up for Mama!" she cooed, and he eagerly formed a circle with his adorable mouth. He'd just started on solid foods and couldn't get enough of them. Just like his Dada, he had a hearty appetite. My mother said he was a spitting image of me. He is. A handsome little dude. The same swag of dark brown hair, baby blue eyes, and dimpled smile. And for a small baby, he was rather endowed. Our pediatrician said he's very advanced for his age. Thank you very much, genes. I fucking loved this kid. Scout, as promised by Tessa, turned out to be the best dog ever when it came to kids. From the day Leo came home from the hospital, he stayed close to him and protected him. Many times I've thought about Sister Marie's words and believe he is indeed our guardian angel. Thank you very much, God. I fucking loved this dog. Please pardon my language.

There was another reason Scout always stayed close to Leo. Our baby was now a major food and toy supplier. I silently chuckled as I watched him sit patiently by Leo's high chair waiting for his cereal bowl leftovers. Or for his pacifier to fall to the floor. A pacifier to Scout was what a Cuban cigar was to me. A treat. And because he chewed them up, we had to order cases of them. It was pretty hilarious watching Scout prance around the house with a pacifier in his mouth. Leo thought it was a hoot, too, and always giggled.

Though it was a special day for both of us, neither Jen nor I had big plans. We decided to stay in with Leo and Scout and order dinner in from our favorite sushi joint. Plus we loved our new house, which we'd moved into just before Leo was born.

It was everything we wanted. Our dream house on Adelaide, a few minutes walk to the Santa Monica stairs and oceanfront promenade, where I respectively worked out and walked Scout. Though you couldn't call it small, it was nothing like my parents' gated palatial twenty-five thousand square foot nouveau riche mansion. It dated back to the thirties and needed a little fixing up, the same family having lived in it forever.

But we both loved it. Me because of the location. And Jen, because it reminded her of the stately Des Moines houses where she grew up. A five thousand square foot Georgian brick colonial with a huge bay window that overlooked the front lawn and sidewalk. It also had a huge yard. Over time we would renovate it, adding a pool and a guesthouse for Jen's parents to stay in. For now, it was perfect and Jen had begun to furnish it with a combination of flea market finds and contemporary artwork. And a few antiquey things my mother gifted us. *The Kiss*, the painting I'd bought her from Jaime Zander's gallery, now hung proudly in our entryway and made me horny every time I stepped through the front door. And on the console we'd brought from my former condo (one of my few bachelor pad furnishings Jen let me keep), there were numerous family photos. Of Jen and me. Of Leo. Of Scout. All of us together. They were a reminder that life was precious. Every day, every minute counted. Tomorrow was promised to no one. There wasn't a day that went by that I didn't feel grateful for my wife. My son. And my dog. I was literally one inch away from death had it not been for Scout. If he hadn't taken that bullet for me, I wouldn't be here celebrating my thirty-second birthday with my wife and son. Or with him.

It was just as well we stayed in. It was also the first day of winter, and for the first time in months, it began to rain. I'm talking crazy buckets. It had been ages since I heard rain pitter patter on a roof, and I kind of liked it. With the fireplace blazing, holiday music playing, and all our Christmas and Chanukah decorations in place, the house felt warm and inviting. Like a Norman Rockwell painting.

Leo was napping in his portable crib, and Jen was hanging more ornaments on the handsome tree we'd bought. There were already numerous, festively wrapped presents beneath it. Jen's parents would be flying here in a few days to celebrate the holidays with all of us and my parents. We were hosting a big Christmas Day brunch. Setting down my *Hollywood Reporter*, I caught Scout sniffing around the tree and was worried he might lift a leg.

"Jen, I'm going to take Scout out for a short walk."

"Blake, don't. It's raining too hard. Just let him go out in the backyard."

That was fine by me. But there was one thing we had to do later this morning. Not miss, regardless of the weather. Drive to Cedars together where Scout volunteered as a therapy dog. Soon after he recovered from his gunshot, I enrolled him in a training course called Pet Partners. Both Chase and our former dog trainer Martha gave him a stellar recommendation, and he came out of the intensive ten-week program first in his class. My bi-monthly visits to the hospital gave me great joy, regardless of how it was sometimes so difficult for me to stomach all the sick people, especially the critically ill kids, whose ailments ran from traumatic head injuries to life-threatening cancer. Scout arrived in his SpongeBob raincoat, wearing it proudly for the first time, and I'll never forget the smiles he put on so many patients' faces, from the youngest to the oldest, as he let them pet and cuddle him. It was a good, good day.

In the late afternoon, at Jen's insistence, I also left the house to have a drink with Chase. We'd become good buds, and sometimes shot hoops together or went for a run. He had a dog too, a beautiful chocolate brown Lab rescue named Roxie that Scout had a crush on. I guess he did like brunettes. At five o'clock, Chase picked me up in his Explorer and we headed over to El Torito on Ocean Park Boulevard for happy hour. Over margaritas and nachos, we shot the breeze and he told me the great news that Tessa had gotten into the esteemed veterinary med school at UC-Davis. She would be starting in the fall.

"Holy guacamole! That's awesome!" I clinked my glass against his.

"Yeah. Tess is totally stoked. I'm hoping she'll join me in my practice when she graduates." And maybe join him in holy matrimony, I silently chortled. They had become a couple.

Thanks to Don Springer's diamond pinky ring, which I hocked for thirty grand, all her first-year expenses would be paid for. My wise old man always said there is a silver lining in every nightmare. He's right. I actually planned to cover Tessa's entire three-year tuition. And ultimately establish a scholarship in Scout's honor for underprivileged kids aspiring to become vets. Chase bought another round of drinks and couldn't be more thrilled.

A little smashed and totally happy, Chaseman, formerly Chasehole, drove me home safely. The rain having stopped, he insisted on coming into the house to say hello to Scout, give Leo, who he adored, a ride over his shoulder. And give my wife a hug. I was way over my jealousy. He was no longer a threat to me.

Oddly, all the lights were off, except for those of our Christmas tree, which twinkled in the bay window, next to the lit up candles of our electric menorah. Maybe my tiger and little lion, as I affectionately called him since Leo roared like his Zodiac sign when he was born, had gone to sleep. Using my key, I unlocked the front door and swung it open. The lights flashed on and then . . .

"SURPRISE! HAPPY BIRTHDAY!"

Holy shit! About three dozen people were gathered in the entryway, including Jen who was holding wide-eyed Leo. Among them were my parents, along with Grandma, Luigi, my sister Marcy and my twin nephews. As well as Jen's parents who must have secretly flown in early to celebrate my birthday. Plus, Libby, Chaz, and Jeffrey. Jaime, Gloria, and their twins. My secretary Mrs. Cho and her husband. Vera and Steve along with their son Josh. My favorite SIN-TV porn stars, Pussy and Swell. Chase's main squeeze, Tessa. Dog trainer Martha and her family. Boyd and Attila. Our beloved nanny Blanca. Stoned out Reverend Dooby, who was playing his guitar. And last but not least, Sister Marie and Nemo. How in God's name (no pun intended) had Jen tracked her down? Everyone was wearing goofy birthday hats. Red and white striped with Black Lab silhouettes all around. Even Scout was wearing one and howling as if he were singing along.

Handing off the baby to her mother, Jen flung her arms around me and hugged me hard.

"Happy Birthday, Blake!" She smacked a kiss on my lips.

I was still in shock. "I can't believe you pulled this off!"

"Yes, with a little help from our friends." She gave Chase a conspiratorial wink.

Drinks. Canapés. More drinks. Dinner. Balloons everywhere. All thanks to Jeffrey, one of LA's top party planners, who had also organized our Christmas in July wedding at Jen's parents' house. Everyone ate, drank, and laughed. Including our dog and baby. Both were total party animals!

And then the cake. A frosted monstrosity with multi-color roses from Hanson's. Buttercream on the outside, raspberry filling on the inside. My favorite.

Thirty-two candles flickered as everyone sang "Happy Birthday."

"My love, blow out the candles and make a wish," urged my tiger, who was standing beside me, back to holding our mesmerized son.

I inhaled a deep breath, pondering what I should wish for. Seriously, what does a man who has it all—a beautiful family, great friends, a dream house, an awesome career, a hefty bank account, and let's not forget my enviable good looks and Guinness-worthy big dick—possibly want? I thought hard. There was only one thing.

Eternal good health and happiness for myself, my treasured family, and everyone we know and love. That wasn't too much to ask for, right? With resolve, I blew out all the candles with a sweeping breath from corner to corner.

Cheers and applause all around.

Then suddenly, a loud chorus of eeeews. And a bunch of nose scrunching guests.

I smelled it too. Ugh! Silent but deadly.

I shot the one who dealt it a look. His special gift. He gave me that big goofy smile.

And I smiled back.

I had to love *that* dog.

A NOTE FROM BLAKE

Hey there, all you beautiful readers~

Hope you enjoyed this story! And fell in love with Scout. Just like me and my tiger. Let me tell you, he's the best dog in the world. I repeat. The. Best. Here to stay!

Whoot! Or should I say Woof? I just saw all your online comments and I'm thrilled you did. But I see some of you have a few unanswered questions. Yours truly is here to help.

So, you may be wondering: what happened to Krystal? Long story short, she didn't make it. When she got to Cedars, she was DOA. I got my wish. She's rotting in hell with her scumbag brother. End of.

You may also be wondering: what else did my tiger give me for my birthday?

Actually, she gave me two more presents. Both big and beautiful. The first, one big beautiful blow job that made me come like Mount Vesuvius. The second, a big beautiful framed portrait of Scout and me that she had custom-made. It's now hanging in my office. Oh, and by the way, she loved the diamond and onyx doggie pin

I gave her for our anniversary and keeps it safely tucked away so Scout won't find it and think it's a doggie treat.

She's now after me to get a cat. *Blake, think about all the poor orphan kitties that need a good home.* Does that sound familiar? This time, I've told my tiger to forget it. I already have one pussy in my life that I love. And that purrs after orgasms. I don't want or need another.

My wise old man once told me you have two families in your life—the one you're born into and the one you choose. Lucky me has done well—make that stellar—on both fronts. I was born into a wonderful family and I chose the perfect wife, who gave me the perfect kid. And I chose the perfect dog. Okay, Jen really chose him and she never lets me forget.

They say a dog's a man's best friend. Believe that. Right from the beginning, Scout was. True to the creed of the official Boy Scout oath, he came into our life to love and protect us. There isn't a day that goes by when he doesn't touch us in some way. Be it to humor us with his panty-snatching antics or surprise us with his heroic acts. Just the other day a nasty bee was hovering over Leo and Scout selflessly leaped across the room to take the sting, just like he took a bullet for me. Something I will never forget.

Scout's taught me a lot. About myself. About canines. About life. I don't think there's a stronger bond than that of a dog and his owner. Unlike humans, a dog's love is unconditional. Pure and unadulterated. Their loyalty fierce and unwavering. Have you ever seen a homeless guy on the street with his dog? The dog sits by his side adoringly, heels when he pushes his cart. Dogs don't care if you're rich or poor. Black or white. Straight or gay. Model perfect or ugly as sin. If you live on the street or if you live in a palace. Okay, it's a lot nicer being good looking and living in a palace, but still. They don't discriminate. Sometimes I think what a better place the world would be if we could be more like dogs.

Jen, Scout, and I—and Leo—have a lifetime of fun and adventures ahead of us. Memories to create. Birthdays. Trips. Holidays. And lots more. But sadly, there will come a day when Scout will leave us and go back to the heavenly space from which he was sent. I dread that day and choke up whenever I think about it, but he will live in my heart forever. I will totally always love him.

I'm going to write a book. A memoir.

And I'm calling it *THAT DOG*.

Until next time . . .
I.T.A.L.Y. ~Blake

THAT DOG

SCORCHIN' HOT USA BEST LOOKING AUTHOR
BLAKE BURNS

A NOTE FROM NELLE

Dearest Readers~

Thank you from the bottom of my heart for reading *THAT MAN 8*. I hope you loved reading it as much as I loved writing it. And I hope Scout put a big smile on your face and made you shed a few tears. If you did enjoy it, I encourage you to leave a review at the retailer you purchased it from. Regardless of the length, reviews mean so much to me and help others discover my books.

I look forward to bringing you more *THAT MAN* books in 2021, but in the meantime, Blake and his tiger are featured in my *Unforgettable s*eries. And wait till you see what Katrina, the Spawn of Satan, is up to in these books! Have a dagger nearby!

Coming in early 2021 . . . my next standalone—*Butterfly*—a steamy and suspenseful age gap romance. My most alpha and tortured hero ever! I'm so in love with Roman Hurst and my feisty artist heroine, Sofi! Add it to your Goodreads TBR.

Thank you again for your love and support. It means

the world to me in this challenging world. Stay well, and remember you are the reason I write.

With all my love and appreciation . . .
MWAH! ~ Nelle ♥

ACKNOWLEDGMENTS

A BIG shout to Team Nelle. I could never do this without you.

My betas: Kelly Green, Marti Jentis, Jill Johnson, Kristen Myers, Ilene Rosen, Lisa Sanders, Mary Jo Toth, and Joanna Halliday-Warren.

My amazing cover designer: Arijana Karčić.

My ever so talented teaser and graphics designer: Hayfaah S.

My eagle-eye proofreader: Virginia Tesi Carey.

My forever patient formatter: Paul Salvette/BBebooks.

My tireless Release Blitz organizer and promoter: Candi Kane.

My lovely, always-there-for-me assistant: Kelly Green.

My A-Team: My dear group of supportive writer friends whose names all begin with the letter "A"... Aubrey Bondurant, Auden Dar, A.M Hargrove, Adriane Leigh, Angel Payne, Arianne Richmonde, and Aleatha Romig. I love you all!

My family: For putting up with me and affording me the opportunity to write. I love you guys and owe you lots of dinners!

And finally, my Pepper: You inspired every word. I LOVE you, my sweet fur baby for always being right by my side!

Stay well all!!

MWAH! ~ Nelle ♥

BOOKS BY NELLE L'AMOUR

Secrets and Lies

Sex, Lies & Lingerie

Sex, Lust & Lingerie

Sex, Love & Lingerie

Unforgettable

Unforgettable Book 1

Unforgettable Book 2

Unforgettable Book 3

THAT MAN Series

THAT MAN 1

THAT MAN 2

THAT MAN 3

THAT MAN 4

THAT MAN 5

THAT MAN 6

THAT MAN 7

THAT MAN 8

Alpha Billionaire Duet
TRAINWRECK 1
TRAINWRECK 2

Love Duet
Undying Love
Endless Love

A Standalone Romantic Comedy
Baby Daddy

A Second Chance Romantic Suspense Standalone
Remember Me

An OTT Insta-love Standalone
The Big O

A Romance Compilation
Naughty Nelle

ABOUT THE AUTHOR

I am a *New York Times* and *USA Today* bestselling author who lives in Los Angeles with her Prince Charming-ish husband, twin college-age princesses, and a bevy of royal pain-in-the-butt pets. A former executive in the entertainment industry with a prestigious Humanitas Prize for promoting human dignity and freedom to my credit, I gave up playing with Barbies a long time ago, but I still enjoy playing with toys with my hubby. While I write in my PJs, I love to get dressed up and pretend I'm Hollywood royalty. My steamy stories feature characters that will make you laugh, cry, and swoon and stay in your heart forever. They're often inspired by my past life.

To learn about my new releases, sales, and giveaways, please sign up for my newsletter and follow me on social media. I love to hear from my readers.

Website:
www.nellelamour.com

Newsletter:
nellelamour.com/newsletter

Nelle's Belles:
facebook.com/groups/1943750875863015

Facebook:
facebook.com/NelleLamourAuthor

Instagram:
instagram.com/nellelamourauthor

Twitter:
twitter.com/nellelamour

Amazon:
amazon.com/Nelle-LAmour/e/B00ATHR0LQ

BookBub:
bookbub.com/authors/nelle-l-amour

Email:
nellelamour@gmail.com

Printed in Great Britain
by Amazon